September

Everyone says change is what makes life an adventure. That when you change, you grow, and if you don't change, you'll shrivel up and rot like an old potato.

Well, baloney. The people who get rah-rah over change are always parents and librarians, not kids. Because when kids change, it's really pretty ugly. Three times out of four it means someone's going to get her feelings hurt, or someone's going to feel stupid when the day before she felt just fine. Three times out of four it means someone's two best friends are out of the blue going to start acting silly and giggly and full of secret looks, and nothing that someone can do will make things go back to normal.

It makes me want to cry.

6

"Any girl who has lived through being 11, or hopes to survive that age, will treasure this book."   —*Dallas Morning News*

OTHER BOOKS YOU MAY ENJOY

Agnes Parker...Girl in Progress	Kathleen O'Dell
The Cat Ate My Gymsuit	Paula Danziger
The Girls	Amy Goldman Koss
Last Summer with Maizon	Jacqueline Woodson
Maizon at Blue Hill	Jacqueline Woodson
Notes from a Liar and Her Dog	Gennifer Choldenko
Otherwise Known As Sheila the Great	Judy Blume

Eleven

Lauren Myracle

PUFFIN BOOKS

For Suzybell and Julianne

PUFFIN BOOKS
Published by the Penguin Group
Penguin Young Readers Group, 345 Hudson Street, New York, New York 10014, U.S.A.
Penguin Group (Canada), 10 Alcorn Avenue, Toronto, Ontario, Canada M4V 3B2
(a division of Pearson Penguin Canada Inc.)
Penguin Books Ltd, 80 Strand, London WC2R 0RL, England
Penguin Ireland, 25 St Stephen's Green, Dublin 2, Ireland
(a division of Penguin Books Ltd)
Penguin Group (Australia), 250 Camberwell Road, Camberwell, Victoria 3124, Australia
(a division of Pearson Australia Group Pty Ltd)
Penguin Books India Pvt Ltd, 11 Community Centre, Panchsheel Park,
New Delhi - 110 017, India
Penguin Group (NZ), Cnr Airborne and Rosedale Roads, Albany, Auckland,
New Zealand (a division of Pearson New Zealand Ltd)
Penguin Books (South Africa) (Pty) Ltd, 24 Sturdee Avenue, Rosebank,
Johannesburg 2196, South Africa

Registered Offices: Penguin Books Ltd, 80 Strand, London WC2R 0RL, England

First published in the United States of America by Dutton Children's Books,
a division of Penguin Young Readers Group, 2004
Published by Puffin Books, a division of Penguin Young Readers Group, 2005

7 9 10 8

Copyright © Lauren Myracle, 2004
All rights reserved

THE LIBRARY OF CONGRESS HAS CATALOGED THE DUTTON EDITION AS FOLLOWS:
Myracle, Lauren, date
Eleven / Lauren Myracle.—1st ed.
p. cm.
Summary: The year between turning eleven and turning twelve brings
many changes for Winnie and her friends.
ISBN 0-525-47165-0
[1. Friendship—Fiction. 2. Best friends—Fiction.
3. Schools—Fiction. 4. Family life—Fiction.] I. Title.
PZ7.M9955El 2004
[Fic]—dc21 2003049076

Puffin Books ISBN 978-0-14-240346-4

Printed in the United States of America

ACKNOWLEDGMENTS

A thousand thanks to the usual crew of family
and friends. (*Sappy music to be played in background.*)
I couldn't have done it without you.

Thanks as well to some great folks from Vermont College:
Graham Salisbury, Sharon Darrow, and Catherine Larkins.

Thank you, thank you, thank you to my fabulous editors:
Susan Van Metre, who guided this book through infancy,
childhood, and adolescence; Julie Strauss-Gabel, who
ushered the book into maturity; and Caroline Beltz,
who assisted us all so ably from start to finish.
Each of you deserves a huge hug and a lifetime supply
of Dr Pepper Lip-Smackers.

And, of course, my warmest thanks to Jack, Al, and Jamie.
I love you with all my heart.

Eleven

March

THE THING ABOUT BIRTHDAYS is that everything should go just right, at least on that one day. And so far today has been perfect, even without cupcakes to pass out during lunch. Not in fifth grade, I told Mom. In fourth grade, sure, but not in fifth. The only kid who'd brought birthday cupcakes was Dinah Devine, and that was at the beginning of the year, so she didn't know better. That's one problem with early birthdays: no one knows what'll be cool and what'll be stupid.

March birthdays are better, like mine. And this birthday in particular, because today is March 11, and today I am eleven years old. It'll only happen like this once, which is why it's especially wonderful that everything's been going so well. Waffles for breakfast, crispy but not burned. At school, a heartfelt chorus of "Happy Birthday," with me beaming at the front of the room. (Ignored Alex Plotkin's bit about monkeys and zoos.) And now, back home in our den, I get to hum and bounce on the sofa to my heart's content without Mom putting her hand on my shoulder and telling me to relax. Not that I *could* relax even if I wanted to. Because in ten minutes or possibly less, I'll have arrived at the best part of the entire day. My party!

During art, Amanda and I had planned out the whole evening, from activities to cake to presents. Ms. Straus had let us scoot our chairs together, and we talked while we drew. Lately I've been liking to draw girls hanging by their knees off tree branches, while Amanda tends to sketch cheerleaders doing daring, fantastic jumps.

"I think you should do presents before cake," Amanda had suggested as she shaded in her cheerleader's skirt. "That way people can have time to digest their pizza."

"Plus, that means I'll get to open the presents sooner," I said. I knew that sounded rude, but with Amanda I could say anything.

"What's your top birthday present ever?" she asked. "Your very favorite thing you ever got."

"From my parents or someone else?"

Amanda switched pencils. "I already know your best gift from your parents: your CD player. From someone else."

I claimed the blue pencil and worked on my girl's shorts. "Well, I *love* the heart necklace you gave me last year."

She rolled her eyes like, *go on*.

"Other than that, I'd guess I'd say my crutches." They were old-fashioned wooden crutches with rubber tips, and they were awesome for acting out stories about brave crippled children or amputees. I'd found them when I was helping my aunt Lucy set up for a garage sale, and she let me keep them as a thank-you-slash-early-birthday-present.

"The crutches are great," Amanda acknowledged, "but what I got you this year is even better." She grinned at my expression. "I can't wait until you see!"

I couldn't wait either, which made me think of another terrific thing about March 11. This year it fell on a Friday, which meant I got to have my party on the exact day of my birthday. Last year it fell on a Wednesday, and the following weekend I had a haunted-house birthday even though it obviously wasn't Halloween. Mom made a cake shaped like a ghost, and my sister Sandra dressed up like a witch and stirred a pot of witch's brew down in the basement. It was really a pot of dry ice we got from Baskin-Robbins, but the steam made it look spooky, and Dinah Devine screamed and got the hiccups and had to be taken upstairs. Then my little brother Ty wet his pants and started to cry.

Another good thing: Mom's paying Sandra ten dollars to take Ty to Chuck E. Cheese, his favorite place in the world. He could spend eons there.

From the window, I saw a blue Honda pull into the drive-way. I scrambled off the sofa and called, "Mom, get down here!" I opened the front door and ran to greet Amanda, who was carrying a medium-size box wrapped in bright green paper. "Amanda! Finally!"

Amanda twisted away with her present, which I was trying to wrest free. "Hands off," she said.

"What is it?" I begged.

"Oh, like I'm going to tell you." She poked my shoulder. "My mom wants to talk to your mom."

"Why?"

"She just does."

We went inside, and I leaned on the railing of the staircase while Amanda put her present in the den. "Mom!" I yelled. "Mrs. Wilson needs you!"

"Winnie, please," Mom said. "I'm right here." She clopped down the stairs in her low-heel shoes. "Hello, Amanda. I like that shirt you're wearing."

I looked at Amanda's shirt—white with purple stripes— and for a second I wished I'd worn something other than my McDonald's shirt with a picture of a Big Mac on the front. *Oh, well.* Another car pulled into the drive, and Amanda and I dashed back out.

"It's Chantelle," Amanda said. She waved. "Chantelle, hi!"

Chantelle is Amanda's and my second-best friend. We met her on the first day of third grade, when Mrs. Katcher tried to guess what everyone's name was. Mrs. Katcher kept frowning at Chantelle and trying new names, until finally she put down her roll book and said, "Sweetheart, I give up! There aren't any more boy's names left!"

Amanda and I found Chantelle during morning recess

and told her Mrs. Katcher was crazy. Didn't she know girls cut their hair short, too? We told Chantelle she looked sophisticated, like a model, and Chantelle smiled and lifted her head from her arms.

Now Chantelle's hair reaches almost to her shoulders, and today she held it back with a big, silver barrette that matched her silver earrings. She handed me a small box wrapped in shiny red paper and said, "Here. Happy birthday."

"Thanks," I said. "I'll put it inside with Amanda's."

Chantelle bumped Amanda's hip. "Is it . . . you know?"

"Is it *what?*" I demanded.

"Yes, but shhh," Amanda said. To me, she added, "And don't try to worm it out of her."

"Hi, everyone!" called Dinah Devine as she struggled out of her dad's station wagon. She wore a bright pink party dress, and her hair was pushed back with a matching plastic headband. Her smile stretched too wide across her face.

"Here," she said. "Happy birthday." She held out her present, a lumpy package tied with yarn.

"Thanks," I said. Dinah is somebody I try to be nice to at school, but I wouldn't have invited her to my party except Mom said I had to. Her dad works with my dad, which in Mom's mind meant Dinah should be included.

But along with her too-wide smile, Dinah is one of those people who laughed too late when someone makes a joke, or too loud, or too long, like, "Ha, ha! That was so hysterical!" even when the joke was really dumb. And if someone says something mean, like "We weren't talking to *you*," or "You don't even get it, do you?" Dinah never says anything back. Although one time she told our teacher, which was a mistake. Then the kids called her a tattletale, too.

Dinah's mom died when Dinah was a baby, which was really sad. I try to remember that. But sometimes the whole mess of it wears me out.

A car horn honked, and Dinah jumped. We moved to the edge of the driveway, and Louise's mom pulled up with Louise and Karen in the backseat. Louise and Karen are best friends, the kind who wear matching outfits to school and loop identical friendship bracelets around their wrists. Today Louise had on blue overalls and a white shirt, while Karen was wearing white overalls with a blue shirt. Karen trailed Louise up the driveway and smiled as Louise said hello for both of them.

"What now?" Louise said after we went inside and deposited their presents with others.

"Well," I announced, "we have very exciting plans. *Shockingly* exciting. Right, Amanda?"

"Shockingly," agreed Amanda.

I glanced from face to face. "I am pleased to inform you that tonight we will be performing a play written by yours truly. It is a dreadful and chilling play. It's called *The True Tale of Sophia-Maria: A Tragedy*."

Louise frowned.

Dinah looked concerned.

"Who's Sophia-Maria?" Karen asked.

"Sophia-Maria is a girl exactly our age," I said. "She has lustrous black curls and violet eyes, and she never did anyone a moment's harm. But sadly, she is snatched from her home and taken to France, where she becomes a scullery maid for a horrible baroness."

"A scullery maid?" Karen repeated.

Louise sighed in a very loud way. "No offense, but could we *please* not put on one of your plays? You always get to be the heroine, and the rest of us get stuck being butlers or ladies-in-waiting."

"I get to be the heroine because I made it up," I explained. "But you can be the horrible baroness if you want. She's hunchbacked from riding camels, and she lisps."

"I don't want to be the baroness," she said. "I don't want to be anything."

This was a problem with Louise. She could be extremely difficult. I tried to appear agreeable while at the same time indicating with my tone that Louise was being a spoilsport. "Well, what *do* you want to do?"

"We could give each other makeovers," Chantelle said.

"Karen's mom won't let her wear makeup," Louise said. "Not until she's in junior high."

"Maybe that telephone game?" Dinah said. "Where

everybody whispers something into the next person's ear and it comes out all silly?"

"Wait," I said, sensing my plans slip from my grasp. "In the play there's a plague, did I tell you? Sophia-Maria gets horrible boils, and—"

"I know!" Louise said. "Do you still have that electric chair? The one that old lady used to use?"

"What old lady?" Karen asked.

"Mrs. Robinson," I said. "The lady who lived here before us. But—"

Karen's eyes grew big. "She had an electric chair?"

"Not *that* kind," Louise said. "Not where you get electro-cuted. Tell them, Winnie."

I told them how Mrs. Robinson couldn't move around very well because she was, like, ninety years old, so she had an electric chair installed in the back staircase. It's an ugly vinyl chair connected to a steel track, and under the arm of the chair is a button, kind of like a doorbell. When you press it, the chair travels up the track. Or down the track, if you start at the top.

"It's not that exciting," I finished.

"It's better than doing a play," Louise said. She headed for the kitchen, and the others followed. By the time I caught up with them, they were crowded around the foot of the back staircase with Louise perched on the cracked vinyl seat.

"Everyone watching?" Louise asked. She punched the

"start" button, and the chair lurched up the stairs, motor whining. We heard a thunk when the chair got to the top, and Karen shrieked.

"It's okay," Louise called. "It always does that." The motor whirred and down came Louise, sitting proudly like a queen.

"Now you," she said to Karen.

Karen hesitated, then climbed onto the chair. "Like this?" she said. She pressed the button and squealed as the chair started back up the stairs.

"Mrs. Robinson?" I said, raising my voice to be heard over the motor. "The lady who lived here? She was so old she *died* in this house. My sister Sandra was afraid to move in because of ghosts."

That wasn't exactly true. Sandra was just trying to scare me.

"I *think* she died in the electric chair," I said even louder.

"Ooo!" everyone cried.

"Karen, you're sitting on a ghost!"

"Karen and ghostie, sitting in a tree!"

"Hey, I want to sit on the ghost!"

"Me, too!"

"Hurry up, Karen! You're squishing the ghostie!"

Karen climbed down, and Chantelle and Amanda got on to do a partner ride, with Amanda sitting in the seat of the chair and Chantelle balanced on one of the arms. Then

Karen went again, although she still didn't have the hang of it. She kept letting go of the "start" button, making the chair stall out. She giggled each time, and the others yelled, "Karen! Push the *button!*"

Louise reclaimed the chair, and I sat down on the lowest step, wrestling with my disappointment. It wasn't that I wanted to be the boss of everyone, but I'd worked hard on *The True Tale of Sophia-Maria.* I'd seen in my mind how it would be performed, and how afterward, as everybody congratulated me, I would blush modestly and say, "It was nothing. I just like to make stuff up."

And it *was* a heart-wrenching story. Sophia-Maria lost three fingers due to the plague, and the baroness cast her into the street with nothing but a tattered gray shawl. She had no friends, and she wandered the earth singing mournful songs. Finally she was killed by a pack of wild javelinas, and when everyone found out, they felt terrible for not treating her more nicely. The last line of the play, to be delivered by the butler, was, "For the welfare of all children, for the consideration of poor, innocent girls and boys, and for the bettering of your community as a whole, I beg you: BE KIND TO A STRANGER TODAY!"

Louise clunked to a halt at the bottom of the staircase. "*That's* how you do it," she said to Karen.

"Can I have a turn?" Dinah asked.

"No," said Louise.

"Why not?"

"Because."

I roused myself from my slump. Dinah's eyes had a rabbity look to them, and her cheeks were pink.

"Yes, you can have a turn," I told Dinah. "Louise, get off."

"I'm not done yet," Louise said.

"You've gone twice already. You've got to share."

Louise hesitated, then hopped down as if she'd never cared in the first place. "You better not break it," she said to Dinah.

Dinah climbed onto the seat and squeezed her knees together. She pressed the button and off she went.

"Okay," I said when she was done. I slapped my hands on my thighs and stood up. "Everyone's had a turn. Let's go to the kitchen and—"

"Hey!" Louise protested. "Karen and I haven't gone double!"

Chantelle pushed her way forward. "I bet if someone helped me I could do a handstand on the—"

"*My* turn to go next—"

"—not fair, because you already—"

"But don't you guys want to eat?" I asked. "We're going to have pizza, and everyone gets to put on their own toppings."

No one paid attention.

"Amanda?" I pleaded. "Aren't you hungry?"

Amanda stopped arguing, and I could tell she'd finally remembered our plans. She stepped toward me. "I love pizza," she said.

"Me, too," said Chantelle.

Louise put her hands on her hips. "Yeah, but—"

"Come on," I said before she could finish. "Last one to the kitchen is a rotten egg."

Originally Mom wanted to stay in the kitchen to supervise, but I told her no, I could take care of dinner myself.

"Here's how it works," I told everyone. "We've got two crusts. Me and Amanda and Chantelle will make this one, and Louise and Karen and Dinah, you can make the other. The toppings are on the counter, and the sauce is in the blue bowl by the sink."

I pulled Amanda and Chantelle toward the counter. My chest felt lighter now that we were back on track. "What should we do?" I asked. "Green pepper and onion? Or, I know! We could make a smiley face, with pepperoni for eyes and a green pepper for the mouth!"

"Not too much green pepper," Chantelle said. "I don't mind a little, but not, like, all over the whole thing."

"That's why I said for the mouth. There's only one mouth."

A worry line formed on Amanda's forehead, and I stopped talking and followed her gaze. At the end of the counter Louise and Karen were sprinkling cheese onto their pizza while Dinah stood to the side, biting her thumbnail.

"Dinah, why aren't you helping?" I asked.

Dinah pulled her thumb out of her mouth and wiped it on her dress. "Um . . ."

"She doesn't like pepperoni," Louise said. She grabbed a handful of pepperoni slices and scattered them over the cheese.

"So split the pizza in thirds," I said.

Louise mushed the pepperonis into the sauce. "Too late."

Dinah gave a wobbly smile. "I can eat pepperoni. I don't mind."

My heart started beating too fast. "You guys," I said to Louise and Karen. "You can't hog that whole pizza to yourselves."

"Who says we're hogging?"

The silence stretched out. I was afraid I was going to cry, or that it would *look* like I was going to cry, which would be just as bad. Why did Louise have to act so snotty? And why couldn't Dinah handle it on her own?

"Fine," I said. "Come on, Dinah, I'll switch with you."

"Wait," Amanda said. She touched my arm. "I'll go."

Amanda joined Karen and Louise, and Dinah stepped up behind me and Chantelle. "I don't mind pepperoni," she said in a voice that was barely there. "We can put it on if you want."

I didn't answer. I plucked off the pepperoni eyeballs and dropped them into the sink.

"But—" Chantelle said.

"We'll use mushrooms instead," I said. I didn't meet her gaze.

After pizza we had cake, because Mom forgot we were supposed to open presents first, and once she brought the cake out, it was too late to take it back. When everyone was done eating, we moved into the den and settled down on the sofa and the floor.

"That's quite a stash you've got there," Dad said, nodding at the gifts piled up on the coffee table. "Sure they're all for you?"

"D-a-ad," I said. I pressed my palms on my legs and tried to get that birthday feeling back. I reached for the box from Amanda, but she shook her head.

"Mine last," she said.

I picked up the package beside it and read the card: "'Happy Birthday, Winnie. Love, Louise.' And, oh, there's a puppy dog holding a balloon." I held out the card for the others to see, and everyone made oohing sounds like they wished that puppy were right here with us.

I tore the paper from the box. "Body glitter!"

"You are *so* lucky," Amanda said.

"Pass it around," said Louise. I handed it to her, and she uncapped the tube.

Chantelle leaned forward. "Now open mine."

I peeled the paper from her present. "Earrings! They're beautiful!"

"They're clip-ons," Chantelle said, "but you can still wear them once you get your ears pierced."

I took the earrings off the card and put them on. They made my ears feel heavy when I moved my head.

"They make you look mature," Louise said. "Like thirteen at least."

"Clip-ons stretch out your ears," Karen warned.

"Not these," Chantelle said.

"They look very nice," Mom said. She won't let me pierce my ears until I'm twelve, but these she couldn't complain about because they were a gift.

"Here, open this one," Amanda said, pushing Karen's present at me. From inside the box I pulled out a set of Bonne Bell Lip-Smackers in all different flavors. The set included five normal Lip-Smackers, plus one huge one with a cord through the top so I could wear it around my neck. Its flavor was "Dr Pepper," and it smelled exactly like Dr Pepper.

From Dinah I got a scrunchy with gold stars on it. "I made it myself," she said, scrunching the hem of her dress. "I can do it over if you don't like the color."

"No, gold's okay," I said. "Thanks."

Finally, Amanda handed me her present.

"It feels empty," I said.

"Open it," Amanda said.

"Open it!" the others cried.

I ripped off the wrapping paper and lifted the lid from the box. Inside lay a card. "'Happy Birthday, Winnie,'" I read aloud. "'Will you take care of me?'" I peered into the box again. There was nothing there. "I don't get it. Take care of what?"

From the doorway came a squeaky meow. Mom was holding a tiny gray-and-white kitten, its whole body smaller than one of my dad's sneakers. The kitten meowed again, and everyone said, "Ohh!"

I jumped up and ran to Mom. "To keep? Really?"

Mom nodded. "Amanda's mother brought her by when she dropped off Amanda."

I turned to Amanda. "Oh, thank you! Thank you, thank you, thank you!" I took the kitten from Mom's arms.

"She's a girl," Amanda said. "Isn't she adorable?"

"Hi," I said to the kitten. "This is where you live now, okay?" She climbed up my chest and pushed at my neck with her head.

"Happy birthday, squirt," Dad said. He came forward and tousled my hair. "We'll leave you girls alone to enjoy your presents. Holler if you need anything."

He and Mom left the room, and I sat down on the floor with my kitten.

"What are you going to name her?" asked Chantelle.

"How about Socks?" Karen said.

"Or Mittens," said Louise, "because of her teensy white feet. And because it rhymes with kitten."

Chantelle wrinkled her nose. "Mittens the kitten?"

I thought for a moment, then said, "Sweetie-Pie."

"Like Sweet-Pea, Amanda's cat!" said Chantelle.

"Yep. They're sisters."

"Adopted sisters," Amanda said. She grinned.

We watched as Sweetie-Pie licked her back leg. Her tongue made spiky spots on her fur.

"Well?" Louise asked. "Is that all?"

"All what?" I said.

"All the presents."

"Yeah, I guess, but—"

"So what are we waiting for?" She stood up and tightened her ponytail. "Let's go play on the electric chair!"

"Yeah!" said Karen.

"Me first!" cried Chantelle as she dashed for the door.

"Nuh-uh!" Louise said. "It was my idea!"

Their feet pounded the floor as they ran down the hall, everyone but me. I heard the whine of the chair's motor, followed by a burst of laughter. Someone must have tried a new trick. Or maybe whoever it was fell off. I hoped it was Louise.

I held Sweetie-Pie close and rubbed my cheek against hers. "You don't want to ride on that stupid chair, do you?" I whispered. "Huh?"

Sweetie-Pie squirmed free. She padded across the room, sniffing in the direction of the back hall.

"She's so cute," Dinah said, appearing at the door. She knelt and scooped Sweetie-Pie into her arms.

"Why aren't you riding the chair?" I asked. It came out sounding mean, and my face grew hot.

"It's boring," she said. "Plus, Louise won't let me. She says I'm too big."

"Louise is a turd. Anyway, my dad's ridden on it and he's way bigger than you."

She sat down beside me. "It's just a chair."

Sweetie-Pie settled into Dinah's lap. From her chest came a tiny purr.

"She likes you," I said grudgingly.

"I have four cats at home," Dinah said. "Gypsy, Muffet, Buffy, and Katzy. They like to be scratched behind their ears, like this." She demonstrated. "Go ahead. Try."

I scratched behind Sweetie-Pie's ears, and her purrs grew louder. From the hall came another burst of giggles, and Dinah and I glanced at each other. She looked anxious, like she thought I might leave.

"We could try out my new Lip-Smackers," I suggested, shifting my gaze.

"You mean it?" Dinah asked. "They're brand-new."

"They're going to have to get used sometime." I grabbed the Lip-Smackers from the table and lined them up, the fruit-flavored ones first and then the giant Dr Pepper at the end. I chose a white one called Coconut Crazy and smoothed it over my lips.

Dinah pointed to a red one called Strawberry Dream. "Can I try this one?"

"Smell it first to make sure you like it."

She held it up to her nose. "I think I like it. Do you?"

I took a quick sniff. "Yeah. It smells good."

She raised it to her lips, crossing her eyes to keep it in sight.

Today I am eleven, I said to myself. *Eleven years old.* From down the hall I heard Karen yell that she was being squished, followed by Louise calling her a baby. In Dinah's lap, Sweetie-Pie continued to purr. I uncapped another Lip-Smacker—Bursting with Blueberries—and breathed in deep.

April

THE FIRST SATURDAY IN APRIL, Mom let me give her a makeover using my new body glitter and lip stuff. She'd been putting me off for weeks, but finally I got stern and told her it was now or never. I'd already used up almost the whole tube of gold body glitter, I pointed out. And the silver wasn't nearly as pretty.

"Well, when you put it like that," she said, lowering her magazine and following me upstairs. She got out her real makeup for me to use as well, and I don't mean to brag, but afterward even Dad said she looked fabulous.

"I had no idea you owned purple eye shadow," he said to Mom. "And the fake mole is *very* dramatic. Really, Ellen, you should have Winnie do your makeup more often."

"Beauty mark, Dad," I said. "Not 'mole.'"

"Yeah, Dad," said Sandra. She'd wandered into the room and was leaning against the wall. "Get with the program."

Mom rose from her dressing table. She patted her hair, which I'd pinned back with dozens of sparkly butterfly clips. "Pardon me," she said loftily, "but Sam's Club awaits. Shall we, Joel?"

"Is Ty going with you?" Sandra asked.

"He can if he wants to," Mom said.

"I do want to!" Ty called. He ran in from their bathroom, where he'd been playing with Dad's shaving cream. "Can I pick out a treat?"

Sandra stepped back to let Mom pass, then plunked onto Mom's cushioned stool. "Do me," she said.

"Really?" I said. Sandra never let me give her makeovers. She made as if to get up, and I quickly stepped forward. "Um, okay. Sure."

My heart beat faster as I grasped the opportunity in front of me. I studied Sandra's face, then uncapped the silver body glitter. Gold *was* prettier for me and Mom, with our brown hair and brown eyes, but silver was perfect for Sandra. I smoothed some over her cheekbones and across her eyelids. I squinted, then selected a shimmery lip gloss from Mom's makeup tray. I rubbed a dab onto Sandra's lips. Finally, I swooped some of Mom's mascara over Sandra's eyelashes. It was tricky, using that tiny little wand, but I managed not to poke her.

"There," I said.

Sandra frowned at her reflection. "I look like a tramp," she said.

"You do not. You look like a mermaid." I twisted her hair on top of her head, letting a few strands straggle down on purpose. The silver glitter made her eyes look bluer than normal, and with her hair swept up, she no longer looked like plain old Sandra.

"Whatever," she said, pulling away and shaking out her hair. But later that night I saw her practicing hairstyles in front of her mirror, which made me feel good, because it meant she liked my ideas. And on Sunday, out of the blue, she let me borrow her colored pencils, the nice ones that came in a special metal case.

Huh, I thought, pulling a green pencil from the case. This was not the Sandra I was used to. But maybe Sandra's teenage hormones were calming down at last, or maybe she liked me better now that I was eleven instead of ten. Eleven did sound much older. Maybe from now on Sandra was going to be like the big sister in *Veronica the Show-Off,* a battered old paperback I'd bought at a library book sale. That sister had rosy cheeks and a cheerful smile, and she was always hugging her little sister and telling her she was precious.

But by Tuesday afternoon, everything went *splat* back to normal. Like a dead fly falling off the windowsill, only not in a gross way, but more in a "oh yeah, this is the way it always is" kind of way. As in, maybe Sandra liked me sometimes, but the sad truth was that she was a grump, and I shouldn't expect her to be otherwise.

What happened was that we were on our way to the dentist, and Mom did two things that irritated Sandra beyond belief. The first was that someone made a smell, and we all knew it was Sandra, only Sandra got huffy and said it wasn't and could we please talk about something else? And

Mom glanced at her from the driver's seat and said, "Well, Sandra, if you don't want to pass gas, perhaps you shouldn't sit with your legs up like that."

Sandra jerked her feet off the dashboard, which made Ty fall into a fit of giggles and which made me giggle, too, although I tried to control myself, because I knew what it was like to do something embarrassing and have everyone know. Once when I was seven, I went with Amanda to day camp, and I sneezed and a big worm of mucus came out. I didn't have a Kleenex, and I didn't know where the bathroom was, so I just sat there until another girl pointed and said, "Ew, boogers." Finally the camp leader fished a piece of tissue from her pocket, which was nice, but it was too late to do much good.

The second thing Mom did might not have bothered Sandra on its own, but on top of the "passing gas" remark, it was enough to throw Sandra into the tight-lipped, staring-out-the-window stage that meant we'd better leave her alone or else. What happened was that Mom saw a girl on the street that looked like Sandra's friend Jenny, and so she said, "Look, there's Jenny!" Which was a perfectly reasonable thing to do, because it's always exciting to see someone unexpectedly on the side of the street. Except it wasn't Jenny, only nobody realized that until after Sandra had already rolled down her window and called, "Jenny, Jenny!" waving her hand and even bouncing a little in her seat.

"Mom!" Sandra cried when she saw the girl-who-wasn't-

Jenny's face. She scooched down low and kept her eyes straight ahead until we were several blocks away.

So by the time we arrived at the dentist's office, Sandra was glowering as if she'd just stepped in dog poop. She stalked into the waiting area and dropped into a chair at the entire opposite end of the room from Mom.

"Winnie, come sit by me," she said, probably because she wanted someone to be mad with.

I glanced at Mom, then slid into the blue plastic seat next to Sandra's. My legs stuck to the seat, and I made squelching sounds by lifting and lowering my thighs.

Sandra glared at me, and I stopped.

"I hate this place," she said. "It smells like soap. Lena Jackson goes to a dentist where everyone dresses up like they're from *Star Trek*, and if you want, you can watch a movie while they clean your teeth."

"Wow," I said. I would love to go to a dentist like that. Or maybe a *Little House on the Prairie* dentist, which would be a really good theme since that was before kids ate too much candy and instead they just got orange slices. "What do they give out for toys? Little starships and stuff?"

Sandra picked up a worn *Highlights* from an empty seat. She tossed it back. "I do not want Stephanie to clean my teeth. If I get Stephanie, I will scream."

"Why don't you want Stephanie?" I asked. I had Stephanie last time, and she chatted with the receptionist the whole time she worked on me. It was amazing, really, how rarely she actually looked in my mouth.

"She's a sadist. She makes my gums bleed. She *enjoys* making my gums bleed."

"Girls," Mom warned, glancing up from her magazine.

Sandra rolled her eyes. She lowered her voice and leaned in close. "And she dyes her hair. Her roots make me want to puke."

The door separating the waiting room from the office squeaked open. "We're ready for you," the receptionist said. She smiled at me and Sandra. "Who's first?"

I looked at Sandra, then unstuck myself from my chair. "I'll go. I don't mind."

"Stephanie's waiting in room two," the receptionist said. "She'll get you all set up."

I heard Sandra snort, but I didn't turn around, because I knew she'd make me laugh. I was sorry Sandra was in a bad mood, but at least I was the one she shared it with.

In the tilt-back dentist's chair, I watched as Stephanie washed her hands and snapped on a pair of rubber gloves. Sandra was right—Stephanie *did* dye her hair. When she sat down to organize her tray of instruments, I could see the dark line of her part. It was interesting, like a stripe. It wasn't something I would have noticed on my own.

"How's school?" she asked, pressing a button that made my chair go back farther.

"Fine," I said.

"Studying hard?"

"Uh-huh."

"That's good. Open up, please."

She went to work on my teeth, poking them with a sharp metal thing and then scraping away with a second sharp metal thing. She told the receptionist about a trip she'd taken to Cumberland Island, and the receptionist said things like "Not me, not in this lifetime," and "Two for one?" and "Well, you'll have to give me the brochure."

While they talked, I thought about the straw Stephanie used to suck up my spit. Really, it was more like a vacuum cleaner than a straw. Or a combination of the two. It tickled, and every so often it made my lip tingle in a way that made me afraid of accidentally jerking away. It was hard, with my mouth open so wide, to lie perfectly still the way I was supposed to.

But what I wondered was where all that spit *went*. Dozens of patients came here every day, and Stephanie used the straw thing on all of them. The end that wasn't in my mouth disappeared into a hole near the tray of instruments, and I suspected there was probably a sink in there. Probably they kept it hidden so that no one would have to see the spit swirling down the drain. Spit could get pretty gloppy, after all. Sometimes when I sat on Ty and tickled him, I let a big ooze dangle out of my mouth. If he wiggled, it would plop off and land on his chest, but if he didn't, it could hang there all day.

Along with the spit question, I also thought about sneezing, which turned out not to be such a good thing. At first I just thought, *what if*. What if I sneezed right as Stephanie was chipping away at a bit of plaque, and she ended up chipping off part of my tooth? Or worse, what if she plunged her scraper into my gums? But then thinking about it turned into worrying about it, and my eyes got watery like a sneeze might actually come. I stared hard at the light shining down on my face and breathed in a shallow way through my mouth until the feeling passed.

Finally, Stephanie raised my chair and told me to rinse. When I spat into the sink, not all of it came free, and I had to use a Kleenex to wipe my mouth. *See?* I told myself. *Gloppy*.

"Are you flossing every night?" Stephanie asked.

"Um . . ."

"You need to floss every night. You had quite a bit of buildup." She handed me a new blue toothbrush in a rectangular box. "All right, you're done. Send in your sister, please."

I hopped out of the chair and headed past the receptionist's desk. As I opened the door that led to the waiting room, I tried to think of something to tell Sandra, something that would make her laugh.

"Your turn," I said when she looked up from her chair. She stood up to move past me, and I said, "Wait! I have to tell you something!"

She looked annoyed. "What?"

"Stephanie's hair. You're right, she dyes it."

"So?"

"So you're right. It looks terrible. And . . . she's gained, like, a hundred pounds."

"Are you kidding me?"

"She's *huge*."

Her lips twitched, and I knew she'd think it was funny even when she saw that it wasn't true.

"Sandra?" Mom said. "They're waiting."

"Thanks for the warning," she said into my ear, then disappeared into the back room.

While Sandra got her teeth cleaned, I played checkers with Ty. The board was falling apart and we had to substitute a penny for one of the pieces, but it was better than reading old *Highlights*.

"King me," Ty said, moving one of his men to the middle of the board.

"No," I said, "you have to get all the way to my side. Remember?"

"King me."

"Ty, no." I moved one of my men.

Ty picked up my piece and placed it on top of his. He

grabbed five more pieces, stacked them up with the others, and rammed the tower with a beat-up yellow truck from the toy bin. "Ka-boom!" he cried.

By the time Sandra was finished, most of the checker pieces had disappeared behind the magazine rack, and Ty and I were using rolled-up *Highlights* to fish them out. I saw Sandra push through the door, and I jumped up and ran over.

"Did she make your gums bleed?" I asked.

Sandra pulled down her lower lip, and I saw dots of red where her gums met her teeth.

"Ew," I said.

"Do you know what she said? What her *only* comment was?"

"What?"

"That if I flossed more, my gums would toughen up. Yeah, that's just what I want—tough gums."

Mom and Ty joined us at the door, and all four of us filed back into the main part of the office so that Mom could pay the bill.

"And you were right about her little problem," Sandra went on.

I giggled.

"Or rather her *big* problem, I should say."

"Sandra, what on earth are you talking about?" Mom asked, uncapping a pen.

"Nothing," Sandra said. "Stephanie happens to have gained a lot of weight, that's all. She must have a disorder. It's really sad."

"And she dyed her hair super, super blond," I added. I stifled my giggles. "It really is sad."

Mom looked startled. "Goodness," she said.

The receptionist returned from the computer and handed Mom the bill. As Mom wrote the check, Stephanie came out of the back room and said, "Sandra, I'm glad you're still here. You forgot your toothbrush."

Sandra froze, then moved quickly to take the toothbrush before Mom could react. But it was too late.

"Why, Stephanie," Mom exclaimed, "you're as skinny as a stick! The girls told me you'd put on weight and dyed your hair!"

Stephanie's eyes widened. "Excuse me?"

"Uh, thanks," Sandra said, snatching the toothbrush. She backed through the main office and dashed through the waiting room, me at her heels. We took the elevator to the main floor, laughing in a way that made me feel giddy.

"Oh my God," Sandra said when we reached the parking lot. "I can't believe Mom said that. Stephanie is going to *kill* us next time!" She raised her eyebrows and pretended to be Stephanie. "Oh dear, did that hurt? Better start flossing!"

"She'll use that little whirring brush, and she'll turn it on high. And she won't let us spit!"

Mom and Ty emerged from the front of the building. Sandra saw them and stopped laughing. She crossed her arms over her chest.

I hesitated, unsure, then said, "Mom, what were you thinking? Stephanie's going to hate us forever!"

Mom unlocked the door to the station wagon. "It popped out. I'm sorry. But if you girls hadn't made up such a lie in the first place—"

"Oh, sure, blame it on us," Sandra muttered.

"Yeah," I said. "Blame it on us when she pulls our teeth out accidentally on purpose and forgets to give us any Novocain!"

Mom got into the front seat. "Winnie, help Ty fasten up. And both of you, stop overreacting." She started the car. "Although Stephanie did insist on being scheduled for your next checkups. I heard her tell Mary Ann."

"Mom!" I wailed. I waited for Sandra to make Mom stop teasing, but with Mom in the game, Sandra no longer wanted to play. She sat stony-faced for the whole ride home, and as soon as we pulled into the garage, she got out of the car and strode to the house.

"Sandra, wait!" I called, untangling myself from my seat belt.

"Winnie, leave her alone," Mom said.

"But—"

"Sandra is angry because she wants to be angry. It's not your job to make her feel better."

I closed my mouth, but I knew Mom was wrong. It *was* my job. I'm her sister.

"Want to play demolition derby?" Ty asked me as Mom helped him out of the car.

"That's a kid's game," I told him. "It's boring." But I couldn't think of anything else to do, so I handed Mom my toothbrush and reluctantly said okay.

That night, I made Sandra a snack of peanut butter crackers and M&M's. I didn't know if she was still mad, but I figured she probably was since she'd sat through dinner without saying a word. I went upstairs and knocked on her door.

"It's me," I said.

"What do you want?"

"I brought you a snack."

She unlocked the door and pushed it open. She took the plate, then raised her eyebrows like, *Yeah? And?*

"Can I come in?" I asked.

"I guess." She sat down on her bed and nibbled on a cracker, watching as I stepped into her room. "Close the door. God."

"Sorry."

She scooted back and leaned up against her pillow. "Today totally sucked. Mom is *such* a pain. And that broccoli she made for dinner was disgusting."

I sat carefully on the foot of the bed. It made me uneasy

when Sandra talked about Mom like this—not that I wanted to leave. But I figured it was a teenage thing, insulting your parents, and I had two more years to go before I'd understand. Anyway, I liked the broccoli, because of the cheese sauce. Pretty much anything tastes good with cheese sauce.

"And Angie called about an hour ago," Sandra went on. "Guess what she's decided to do?"

"What?" I said. Angie was one of Sandra's best friends. Sometimes she painted my toenails and used those spongy things to separate my toes while the polish dried.

"She's going out for cheerleading. Can you believe it? She asked if I wanted to be her partner for the tryouts."

I could tell by Sandra's expression that the answer had been no, which was too bad. Having a sister who was a cheerleader would be fun. Like having a sister who was a movie star.

But I said, "That's crazy," and Sandra nodded and rolled her eyes.

"Tomorrow she's going shopping for her tryout outfit," she said. "It has to be green and white. Her sister Nina is going to lend give her a pair of socks from when she was a cheerleader, little white ankle socks with green paw prints on them. Isn't that the dumbest thing you've ever heard of?"

"Paw prints?" I said. They sounded the tiniest bit cute, but that was probably because I hadn't seen them. I slid my hands under my thighs. "So, um, you think she'll make the squad?"

"Who cares?" Sandra said. She closed her eyes. "That's awful. I don't mean that. It's just . . ." She opened her eyes and stared at the ceiling. "Angie and I, we're not even that good of friends anymore. I think I've outgrown her."

I blinked. Was that possible? *Could you really outgrow a friend?*

"What do you mean?" I asked.

"All Angie wants is to be popular. It's boring."

I must have looked worried, because Sandra sighed and made a fluttering motion with her hand. "We've grown apart, that's all. It happens."

Not to me, I thought. *Not with Amanda.* Still, I tried to act mature. "Oh. Right. Does Angie care?"

The question surprised her, I could tell. But she frowned and said, "Don't be dumb." She moved the snack plate and sat up. "Go do something else. I've got stuff to do."

"Like what? I could do it with you."

"Leave," Sandra said.

I got off the bed and leaned against the bedpost. "Can I borrow your Sunkist shirt?" I asked. I loved that shirt. It was a soft, faded orange. On me it hung low enough to be a nightshirt, and when I wore it, I pretended I was going to a slumber party.

"No," Sandra said.

"Please?"

"I said no."

I walked to the door. I dragged the toe of my sneaker against the carpet.

"Oh, all right," she said. She jerked open the middle drawer of her dresser and tossed me her Sweet Treats shirt instead. "Just don't get it dirty."

"Thanks," I said, backing into the hall as she shut the door. Her Sweet Treats shirt wasn't as good as her Sunkist shirt, but it was close. On the front were the words SWEET TREATS ICE-CREAM PARLOR, and on the back were two smiling ice-cream cones. On the bottom of the shirt, way down low where you could hardly see it, was a small, round hole. Sandra made it with a cigarette, she told me. Someone handed her one at a party, and she took it because she didn't want to be rude. But she didn't smoke it. She stretched a bit of the shirt between her fingers and held the cigarette to the fabric, just to watch it burn through.

May

So WHAT DO YOU WANT TO DO?" I asked Amanda. She'd come home with me from school, and for half an hour we'd lounged against the kitchen counter, eating Chee•tos and wiping the orange dust on our shorts. But we were getting bored. "Want to get my pogo stick and see who can jump the most?"

"Only if you want to have a throwing-up contest afterward and see who can throw up the farthest," Amanda said. She dipped her hand back into the Chee•tos bag.

"We could go bird catching," I suggested. Dad once told me that if I caught a bird, I could keep it. He said it in a ha-ha kind of way, like I never would, and I couldn't wait to see his face when I marched into the house with a thrush cupped in my hands. The thrush would have soft brown feathers and trusting brown eyes, and I'd name her Midge. Or Brownie.

Amanda assumed an all-purpose phony accent and said, "I theenk not, my dear." She gestured at her shorts. "Ze grass stains? My mother would keel me."

I considered pointing out the Chee•tos stains already there, but I kept my mouth shut. It was fun to think about catching a bird, but, to be honest, the actual event meant a lot of pouncing, which could be painful. Plus there was all that whispering, which started off giggly but grew bickerish and more blaming as the afternoon wore on.

"Let's walk to Keeng's," Amanda said. It was really King's she was talking about, as in King's Drugs, but she was still using her accent. She pushed herself away from the counter. "We can try out ze perfume samples."

"Okay," I said, "but only if ve go to Reechard's, too." King's and Richard's are plunked smack-dab next to each other in Peachtree Battle Shopping Center, which is a little strange since they're both drugstore-y types of stores. I guess it's okay, though, because they sell different stuff. King's sells makeup and perfume and magazines—normal drugstore things—while Richard's is packed with weird junk like old metal lunchboxes and Styrofoam rabbits. One time I bought a pair of green plastic sunglasses with square lenses, like something a space alien would wear.

I rolled up the Chee•tos bag and put it back in the pantry, then yelled to Mom where we were going.

"What?" she called. "I can't understand a word you're saying!"

This made Amanda and me giggle, so it was a few seconds before I called up to her again, this time without the accent.

Then Amanda and I banged out the door, and just being outside made everything seem lighter and more interesting.

"Come on," I said. I pulled her down the driveway, and as
we turned right onto Habersham, I got the idea of pretending to be orphan girls on the run. This meant we had to
walk very fast and every so often glance over our shoulders,
because we'd just escaped from an evil orphanage.

"Where our clothes were made out of burlap, and all we
ate was gruel," Amanda said.

"And we only got one cup of water a day," I said.

"Except when visitors came, because then the orphanage
lady served hamburgers," Amanda embellished. "Only really
they were made out of rat. And all of the kids knew it,
because she told us, like 'heh, heh' in this really nasty voice.
And then she laughed and rubbed her hands together, but
we had to eat it anyway or she'd lock us in the basement.
The *dungeon*. And all the visitors would walk by and say,
'Oh, how sweet, they get hamburgers here like real children.'
And we'd be gagging, but the orphanage lady would just
laugh and say, 'No manners at all, the poor dears. They were
abandoned when they were two, you know.'"

I imagined those poor two-year-olds, now older and being
forced to eat rat meat, and I thought how great it was that
Amanda could come up with this stuff. Chantelle couldn't.
She always wanted us to be models, or sometimes Xanadu
Maidens, which were like models only on Rollerblades. But

Amanda and I could make up stories for hours. Once we played Lost on a Desert Island for an entire night and all the way through to the next morning.

I heard a car coming, and I grabbed Amanda's arm. "Hurry, dear sister, we must hide!" I said. "If we're found, we will surely be beaten!"

We ducked behind a boxwood. Amanda peeked around the leaves and cried, "It's George, the orphanage lady's son! Oh, no, he saw me! Run!"

We ran down the street, laughing at the startled looks we got from people in their cars. Then suddenly there were popping noises all around us, like firecrackers, and I screamed and covered my head. Amanda screamed, too, and a blue pickup revved its motor and zoomed up the hill. The sound of boys' laughter trailed behind.

"Are you okay?" I asked Amanda. Her face was pale, except for her freckles.

"Yeah. Are you?"

"I think so."

Cautiously, we walked back to the place where the truck had passed us. I knelt and picked up a curled piece of cardboard. It looked like a burned match.

"Snap 'n Pops," Amanda declared. "My cousin had them at the beach last summer."

The curled pieces were all over the road. Tons of them.

"They threw Snap 'n Pops at us?" I said. My heart was

still racing, but now that it was over and the boys were gone, I got a feeling of wanting to laugh. I looked up the hill, and then I looked at Amanda. We cracked up, and once we started, we couldn't stop.

"They must have been George's evil cousins," Amanda said.

"His henchmen," I said. "Death by Snap 'n Pops!"

We laughed longer than we officially had to, stumbling down the hill and bumping each other with our shoulders. If Amanda started to peter out, I'd say "Snap 'n Pops" in a threatening manner, and off she'd go again. Or if it was me who began to lose steam, she'd throw her hands over her face and cry, "I've been blinded! Aaagh!" It was the kind of laughing where one burst led to another and another, and our breath got all gaspy and hilarious. I wanted it to last forever.

In the makeup aisle at King's, I searched for a giant-size Lip-Smacker to replace the Dr Pepper one Karen had given me for my birthday. I'd loved that Lip-Smacker, and now it was gone, because Ty had found it and eaten it. On the shelf before me I saw regular-size Lip-Smackers, as well as Blistex and Carmex and cherry-flavored Chap Stick, but that was it.

I wandered back to the perfume section, where Amanda was spraying herself with a perfume called Sand and Sable. She sniffed the damp patch of skin, then held out her arm. "What do you think?"

I smelled her wrist. "Ick," I said. "Come on, let's go to Richard's."

"Not yet," Amanda said. "I want to check out the magazines. They have the new *Seventeen*. Did you see?"

I groaned. I didn't care about the new *Seventeen*. I got a brainstorm and grabbed her arm. "We don't have time," I said. "It's George—he's heading this way."

"Who?"

"You know, *George*. The orphanage lady's son. We've got to hurry!"

Amanda pulled her arm away. Her eyes flicked to the lady behind the counter. "Winnie, not now."

"Yes, now! I saw him two aisles over, standing in front of the razor blades!"

"No, I mean—" She bit her lip, and I realized with a flush of heat that she was embarrassed.

"I was kidding," I said, loud enough for anyone nearby to hear. "Jeez. It's just that it's so boring in here."

"I know," Amanda said. "I just need a few more minutes, really. You go on to Richard's, and I'll meet you there."

"Fine," I said. I stood there for a minute, but she didn't change her mind.

At Richard's, I walked purposefully down the aisles so that anyone watching would know that this was a *very interesting* store and I was *very interested* in everything. In the back corner, I stopped in front of a shelf of plastic containers. Next to the containers was a shelf filled with ceramic cats and dogs. The cats and dogs were cute, but the containers had more possibility. For example, there was a sky-blue container that would be perfect for holding sea glass, if I happened to have a sea-glass collection. Last year there was a girl in my grade who used to live in Florida, and for her science project she brought in a piece of poster board with bits of sea glass taped all over it—smooth hunks of glass that looked like pieces of the ocean.

I picked up a pink container and tugged on the lid. It made a popping sound when I pulled it free, and when I put it back on, it snapped into place with a thunk. This container would be perfect for storing treats in, I thought. Like Gummi Bears or Hershey's Kisses. You would see the candy through the side of the box, and it would make your mouth water, so that the candy would taste all the better when you finally plunked a piece in your mouth.

Last year at Christmas we had Secret Santas in homeroom, and the person I got paired with was that same girl from Florida, the one with the sea glass. Her name was Mindy. I bought a plastic box like this one, only smaller, and I painted her name on it with puff paint. I added little flowers and one buzzing bee, and I threw in some wavy lines above the bee's wings so that it looked like the bee was actually flying. Then I filled the box with miniature Reese's cups. The day after I gave it to her, she came up to me and said, in an annoyed sort of way, "My mom told me not to tell you, but I'm allergic to peanut butter. Just so you know."

This year Mindy moved back to Florida. Ha-ha-ha-ha-ha.

An old lady doddered down the aisle, sending all thoughts of Mindy from my mind. I clutched the plastic box and stared. The lady's white bun was loose and floppy, like a drifting bird's nest, and her neck was so wrinkled that folds of flesh hung over the collar of her dress. And she had a weird smell. Like baby powder mixed with petroleum jelly. She did something with her lips that made a smacking sound, then lifted a wavering hand to one of the ceramic cats.

She couldn't reach it. Her hand shook as she tried again, and then she turned toward me. I panicked. I shoved the box on the shelf—not where it belonged, but too bad—and darted to another part of the store.

Once I was safe in the toy section, a wave of shame washed over me. I hadn't run because I didn't want to help; I'd run because she was too old. Freaky old. But everyone got old eventually, unless they died first, and who wanted that? One day *I* would be old. Did I want kids to run screaming when they saw me?

My heart was thumping in a way I didn't understand. I glanced around and tried to get interested in the rows of toys. On one shelf sat dozens of troll dolls with crazy hair. On another was a bunch of G.I. Joe stuff, all rifled through and cluttered so that none of the packages faced the right way. At the end of the shelf was a pair of pink strap-on roller skates, flimsy and cheap. I couldn't imagine anyone buying them, unless she knew she'd never have enough money for real Rollerblades.

Amanda and I both had Rollerblades. Amanda's were nicer than mine, but neither of us cared. When we were in third grade, we used to talk about how we'd live together when we grew up, and how we'd have a big house with wooden floors so we could Rollerblade whenever we wanted.

I know now what a dumb idea that was, but I still like to think about it sometimes. When Amanda got here, I'd ask if she remembered. Or maybe not. I flashed on Amanda's expression back at King's perfume counter. I didn't want her thinking I was a baby.

I wondered if the old lady I'd run from had had a best friend, and if they were still friends now. I wondered what they talked about. Or what if the lady *did* have a best friend, but that friend was dead, and now she had no one? I imagined her in a cluttered apartment, watching the *Wheel of Fortune* with the sound turned off. She probably ate TV dinners, or ravioli from a can. For dessert, a crusty Fig Newton.

I returned the roller skates to the shelf. I chewed on my thumbnail, imagining growing older and more alone. Imagining no Amanda.

I walked to the front of the store, not knowing exactly what I was going to do but wanting to do something. I hesitated at the card section, then picked out a yellow card with a bouquet of flowers on the front. Inside, it said: TO A VERY SPECIAL PERSON. I took the card to the cash register and paid for it with two crumpled dollar bills. I stuck the card in the envelope, licked the flap, and pressed it shut.

My stomach got jumpy, but I made myself walk to the ceramic-cats-and-dogs aisle. No old lady. I searched for her in the aisle with the sewing stuff, and then farther up near a display of kitchen timers. There she was, squinting at a timer shaped like an egg. I came up behind her and took a breath. I reached out to tap her shoulder.

"Winnie?" Amanda said.

I whipped around and saw her behind me. She'd come in without my noticing.

"Find anything good?" she asked.

My pulse thudded, and I jammed the card into the waistband of my shorts. "Not really," I said. "What about you? Did you buy any perfume?"

"Too expensive. I bought the new *Seventeen,* though." She held up her brown bag. "We can look at it later if you want."

I shrugged. My palms felt sweaty. I stuck my hands behind my back.

"Anyway, I'm sorry I took so long." Her eyes slid to a canister of magnets. "And I'm sorry for acting . . . you know. Kind of weird a while ago."

Now she was the one who blushed, and I knew it'd been

hard for her to say. Even for best friends, sometimes things can be hard.

"That's okay," I said. "I'm sorry, too—for acting so dumb. Sometimes I just do stupid things."

"You don't. *I* do."

"No, *I* do."

I felt the edge of the card pushing against my skin, and I pulled it out.

"Here," I said, before I could change my mind.

"What's this?" She opened it, and her eyebrows went up. "'For a very special person'?"

"Well, you are," I said.

She gazed at me, then grinned and bumped my shoulder. "You are so *strange*," she said.

And then it was fun, because for the whole walk home, we were both super nice to each other. Like, when we got to the crosswalk, I gestured to the street and said, "After you," and she said, "No, you," and I said, "No, you," and on and on until the light turned red and we had to wait for it to change again. About half a mile from my house, Amanda went back to playing orphans, which I went along with even though I knew she was only doing it because there was no one else around. We belted out the lyrics to "Tomorrow," which for an orphan is especially heart-lifting, but even in our happiness we made sure to keep an eye out for evil George. For all we knew, he could be lurking anywhere.

June

ON THE LAST DAY OF SCHOOL I wore my best pair of jeans and a soft, white shirt with a butterfly on the front. Amanda wore new overalls, and Chantelle wore a pink tank top and a denim miniskirt. We'd dressed up on purpose, because that afternoon the entire fifth grade was going to Jellybeans for an ice-skating party. It was going to be great.

"Just think," Amanda said during homeroom. "After today we'll no longer be fifth graders."

"That's right," said Chantelle. "After today, we'll be in the sixth grade. *We'll* be the sixth graders."

"There'll be no one above us," Amanda said.

"We'll *rule!*" they said together.

I cleared my throat. "Actually," I said, "we won't be sixth graders *yet*. Not technically."

"What are you talking about?" Amanda asked.

"Well, we won't be fifth graders anymore, but we won't be sixth graders, either, because we won't be *in* the sixth grade."

Chantelle rolled her eyes.

"Not until September," I said stubbornly. I'd thought about this a lot, the gap between one grade and the next. During the summer, if some grown-up asked what grade I was in, I always took the time to give the exact, honest answer. Otherwise I felt like a liar.

"Maybe you won't be a sixth grader," Chantelle said, "but I sure will, and I can't wait."

"I can't wait for the party this afternoon," Amanda said, pulling us back to the real issue. "I haven't been ice-skating in forever."

"Me neither," said Chantelle. "Not since my cousin's birthday party." She fingered the strap of her tank top. "Do you think I'll be too cold in this? Maybe I should have brought a jacket."

"You'll warm up once you start skating," Amanda promised. She poked Chantelle in the ribs. "Or maybe Tyrone will keep you warm."

Chantelle blushed. "Oh, please."

"You *are* going to ask him, aren't you? During girls' pick?"

"Girls' pick" was when they played a slow song over the speakers, and if you wanted a guy to skate with you, you had to go up and ask him. The three of us got giggly just thinking about it.

"If I ask Tyrone, then you have to ask someone, too," Chantelle said.

"Don't count on it," Amanda said.

"Winnie?"

My mind flashed to shy Toby Rinehart, who hardly ever talked, but was really good in art. I doubted I'd have the nerve to ask him, but who knew?

"I don't even know how to skate to a slow song," I said.

"You just hold hands and . . . *skate*," Chantelle said.

"Guess you'll have to show us," Amanda teased.

"Maybe I will!"

Ms. Meyers walked in from the hall and shut the door. "All right, class, time to settle down," she said. "I know you're excited about this afternoon, but we have a lot of work to do before then. Turn in your math books to Chapter Twenty-four, and Mark, would you do problem number five on the board?"

I pulled out my book and opened it on my desk. I drew a jelly bean at the top of the page, but it looked dumb, more like a lima bean or a puddle. To do a really good jelly bean, I'd have to have colored pencils.

I peeked at Toby from under my bangs. I bet he could draw a good jelly bean without even half trying. If he could draw an aardvark—which he did once, during our unit on African animals—then he could definitely draw a jelly bean.

All day long kids got wilder and louder, and the teachers threatened to call off all graduation parties if we didn't get ourselves under control. But we knew they wouldn't. During music, Robert used his recorder to shoot spitballs into Karen's hair, and during language arts, Karen got him back by hiding his notebook under a bunch of magazines in the reading corner. He was definitely her choice for girls' pick. It was obvious.

During lunch, Alex Plotkin shook David's Coke up under the table so that it sprayed all over David's face when he popped it open. Then David flicked a scoop of applesauce into Alex's hair, and another into his ear.

"They are so immature," Chantelle said from our table at the other end of the cafeteria. She opened her pack of Oreos and gave one to me and one to Amanda. "I can guarantee no one will ask them to skate during the slow songs."

"Maybe they'll ask each other," I said. "And you know what they'd do. They'd go around slamming into everyone and making kissy noises."

Chantelle scowled. "They better not. That would be just like them, to ruin it for everyone else."

Amanda took a bite of her carrot stick. "David's not so bad by himself," she said. "Once, when Alex was absent, he helped me set up my science project. He was really sweet."

"Yeah, David can be okay," Chantelle admitted.

"But Alex," I said. We looked at one another and burst out laughing.

"Uh-oh," Amanda said. "Here comes Mrs. Jacobs. Now they're going to get it."

Mrs. Jacobs is the assistant principal. She is really pretty, and she makes a point of asking how things are going when she sees us in the hall. On Wednesday afternoons, she led a group for kids whose parents were divorced, and Katie Jacobson said she was super, super nice. Katie said she could even get Alex to act like a human being, which sounded extremely unlikely to me. But I wasn't in the group, so I didn't know.

Mrs. Jacobs frowned when she saw Alex and David's mess, but she didn't go over and stop them. She scanned the room and headed instead toward our half of the cafeteria. Toward our table. Toward us.

"What does she want?" Amanda whispered.

"I don't know," Chantelle whispered back.

"Hello, girls," Mrs. Jacobs said, standing before us. She wore a blue suit with a narrow skirt, and she looked very official. Like a cop.

"Hi, Mrs. Jacobs," we said.

"I like your suit," Chantelle said.

"Thank you, Chantelle. I like your outfit, too." She smiled. "Are you all looking forward to the skating party?"

We nodded.

"Are you coming?" Amanda asked.

"I'm afraid not. I'll be at the square dance, saying good-bye to the sixth graders. Next year, it will be you who will be leaving us."

We sat quietly, letting that sink in. It gave me goose bumps.

Mrs. Jacobs tilted her head. "Winnie, may I talk to you for a moment?"

I glanced at Amanda and Chantelle, then scooted back my chair. Together, Mrs. Jacobs and I walked to her office.

"Am I in trouble?" I asked. I couldn't imagine what I might have done, unless she thought I was the one who hid Robert's notebook.

"No, no," Mrs. Jacobs said. She opened the door to her office and gestured toward a chair. "I have a favor to ask, that's all. It concerns the skating party."

I sat down.

"It's a bit delicate," she said, "and I'm not even sure I should be interfering. But when a student is going through a hard time, it's our job to help out. Right?"

I stared at her, confused. I wasn't going through a hard time. Behind her, on the wall, was a poster printed with the school's slogan: DARE TO CARE!

She looked at me in the solemn way grown-ups do when they want you to feel as if they're treating you like a real person instead of a child. My neck prickled, because when grown-ups look at you that way, there's always something expected in return.

"You've got a big heart, Winnie," she said. "All your teachers have always commented on how kind you are."

"They have?" I said.

"That's why I thought of you when this problem was

brought to my attention." She drummed her fingernails against her desk, then stilled her hand. "Alex Plotkin is worried that no one will choose him for the girls' pick. I was hoping you might help."

"Oh. Uh . . . how?"

"Well, I was hoping you'd consider picking him. If you want to, that is."

My stomach dropped. I must have gone pale, because Mrs. Jacobs said, "Winnie?"

I couldn't speak. I couldn't even get my brain to work. All I could think was, *Alex Plotkin? She wants me to skate with Alex Plotkin?!*

Mrs. Jacobs furrowed her brow, and I opened my mouth to reply. Then I grew hot as the injustice of the situation sank in. Teachers weren't supposed to ask things like this. Not teachers, not assistant principals, not anyone! It was . . . it was . . . unconstitutional. Even with the "if you want to" tagged on, it was completely unfair. Because of course I didn't want to pick Alex Plotkin. No one in her right mind would pick Alex Plotkin, so to tell the truth, he was right to worry. But that was *his* problem, not mine.

"You certainly don't have to, Winnie," Mrs. Jacobs said. "It's up to you."

My heart got hammery, because this was clearly one of those times when even though she *said* it was up to me, we both knew what I was supposed to do, so the only question was whether I really did have a big heart or if my heart was a selfish, shriveled lump. It was a test, like when Mom asked me to share my Magic Markers with my cousin Shalese, who bore down on them too hard and made the ends all stubbly. Or when Dad told me how much he appreciated my open-mindedness right before serving his carrot-ginger soup, which no one else would try.

But *Alex Plotkin?*

Mrs. Jacobs smiled gently and placed her hand on my knee. "Think about it. That's all I'm asking."

I stood up. "Can I go now?"

"Yes, you can go, but whatever you decide, I'd appreciate it if you'd keep our conversation to yourself." She opened the door for me. "It's going to be a great party. Have fun."

For the rest of the afternoon, I stole glances at Alex when he wasn't looking: Alex making farting noises by jamming his hand under his armpit; Alex calling, "No dogs allowed!" when Dinah walked into the room after recess; Alex ducking his head and sticking his finger up his nose, then quickly pulling it out. I did not want that hand touching mine.

Why did Mrs. Jacobs have to ask *me* to do her favor? Why not Amanda, or even Chantelle? Why not Katie Jacobson, who knew Alex from the divorce group and surely had better reasons to pick him than I did. Why couldn't *she* dare to care?

Mom would be proud. She would explain that Mrs. Jacobs

had faith in me to do the right thing. But I didn't want to do the right thing. I wanted to ask sweet, shy Toby Rinehart to skate with me, not sneaky-nose-picking Alex. And I wanted to ask Toby even more now that there was a chance I wouldn't be able to.

The worst part was that I couldn't even moan and groan to anyone about it, since Mrs. Jacobs had specifically asked me not to. Back in the cafeteria, I'd told Amanda and Chantelle that she had a question about my attendance record, and they'd nodded and returned to discussing the party.

So, during science, when Maxine scooted her chair toward Mark's and let him share her book, I could only sigh. Amanda and Chantelle nudged each other, giggling at the blooming couple, but not me.

From across the room, Alex flipped his eyelids inside out and leered at Keiko, who dropped her test tube and screamed for Ms. Meyers. I buried my head in my arms.

"Aren't you having fun?" Amanda asked as she whizzed by me, her long hair snapping behind her.

"Isn't this *awesome?*" Chantelle echoed, close on Amanda's tail.

I watched them grab hands and whip around the far end of the skating rink, using each other for momentum, while I continued to plod in a pathetic circle a foot and a half from the wooden rail. I could have skated with them if I wanted to, but I was too busy thinking about Alex. Plus, I wasn't as good as they were. The only person worse than me was Dinah Devine, who clutched the rail with both hands while her feet skittered crazily away from her.

I hoped Mrs. Jacobs was having a miserable time at the square dance.

I hoped Alex would throw up from all the grape Pixie Sticks he'd eaten and have to be rushed to the hospital, where they'd pump his stomach and it would come out purple.

I hoped that just this once there wouldn't be a girls' pick, that the lights would never go low and that the music would stay loud and boppy until the party was over. The only problem was that then Chantelle wouldn't get to ask Tyrone to skate, and I knew she really wanted to.

Half an hour before the party ended, she got her chance. The lights dimmed, and the disco ball sent soft pastel spots swooping over the floor. The beginning notes of "I Will Always Love You" sent a hush over the room.

"All right, boys," the DJ said, "slick back your hair and polish your blades, because this one's a girls' pick." He sat back and turned the volume higher. "They're all yours, girls. Go get 'em."

I felt sick, sicker even than the time I found half a fly in my pimiento cheese sandwich. Beside me, Amanda squealed and said, "Look! Chantelle's about to ask Tyrone!" She squeezed my arm. "He said yes, he said yes! Oh, look how cute they are!"

Chantelle and Tyrone stepped onto the rink. Pink dots flitted over their bodies like fireflies.

"Oh," Amanda breathed.

Then Karen and Robert stepped onto the rink, and then Maxine and Mark. My stomach clenched tighter. Several more couples glided onto the floor.

I closed my eyes and dug my fingernails into my palms. I didn't *have* to ask Alex to dance. If Mrs. Jacobs ever brought it up, I could tell her I had a stomachache, which was true. Anyway, she wasn't here, so she'd never know what really happened. No one would know but me.

"Why are your eyes closed?" Amanda asked. "Is it the lights? Are they making you dizzy?"

It was no use. If I didn't ask Alex, *I* would know, and I would have to live with it forever. What if Alex grew up to be a deranged maniac, all because he'd been rejected at our fifth-grade party? It wasn't impossible. He already eats live worms. And there's that creepy thing he does with his eyelids.

"I feel like I'm going to throw up," I said. I took in Amanda's concerned expression. Poor, sweet Amanda. "I'll be back, okay?"

I clomped across the carpet to where Alex stood alone by a gray plastic trash can. The remains of some kid's birthday cake sat on a piece of cardboard near the top, the blue-and-white icing melting and beginning to smear. I put my hands on my hips. "Do you want to skate?"

First he looked surprised, and then he changed his mind and smirked. "With you?"

I narrowed my eyes.

"I guess," he said, as if he were doing me a favor.

We wobbled to the rink and stepped onto the floor. His lips were purple from the Pixie Sticks, and the hair near his ear was spiky with dried applesauce. He took my hand, and I pressed my lips together. His palm felt damp and clammy, like a cold hamburger patty.

He lunged forward on his skates, yanking me with him, then jerked backward as he tried to maintain his balance. He was an even worse skater than I was. Worse, even, than Dinah Devine. Better and faster couples passed us on the left, gawking as they sailed by. I hated being the couple that made everyone else feel better.

Chantelle and Tyrone came up on our right and stayed even with us just long enough for Chantelle to say, "Winnie?" as if her eyes had deceived her and surely it wasn't really me.

"It's not!" I wanted to say. "Not really!" But they were gone, skating in sync with their arms around each other's waist.

On our second lap, I saw Amanda staring from behind

the wooden railing. She was standing with the other girls who hadn't asked anyone to skate, and she was talking very fast and shaking her head. I sent her a desperate look, knitting my eyebrows and kind of twitching my head, but I'm not sure she saw because right then Alex tugged on my hand and almost brought us to the floor.

"Come on," he said. "Speed it up!"

"What?" I said.

"You're too slow. Come on!"

That was it. I ground my teeth together and pumped as fast as I could, pulling Alex behind me the way I pulled Ty when he was dragging his heels.

"Hey!" Alex cried.

I heard kids laughing from the sidelines, but I didn't care. I concentrated all my energy on pushing and gliding with my thigh muscles. I almost tripped, but I caught myself and kept going.

The song was almost over. As Whitney Houston's voice rose higher, Alex and I pressed harder and faster around our final lap. Alex was matching my pace now, and we were flying. Our strides were clumsy and our arms flailed in wild, uneven slashes, but we were flying.

Whitney's voice throbbed on the last, impossibly high note of the song. She held it for what seemed like forever, and then the song ended and the normal lights came back on. A new song bounced from the loudspeakers, and kids came pouring onto the rink. I dropped Alex's hand and skated to the exit. I didn't look back.

Later, Amanda found me sitting on the bench by the lockers. "Wow," she said. "I didn't know . . . I mean, I had no idea—" She tilted her head. "Do you like Alex Plotkin?"

"No," I said. "Are you crazy?"

"But you picked him. You asked him to skate with you. He's over at the refreshment stand right now, telling everyone what a huge crush you have on him."

"I do not like Alex Plotkin," I said through gritted teeth. "I was framed."

"What?!" Amanda said.

I told her the whole story, how Mrs. Jacobs pulled me into her office and practically ordered me to choose him during girls' pick. I couldn't help it—I had to tell someone. I made her swear to keep it a secret.

She sat down beside me and rested her chin in her hands. "I think that was very nice of you," she said.

"You do?"

We heard a loud burp, followed by Alex's horsey laugh. We looked toward the drink stand and saw him weaving around with Coke coming out of his nose.

"Extremely nice," Amanda said.

We sat there for several minutes.

"You want to skate some more?" I asked.

"Nah," she said. "Unless you want to. Do you want to?"

I didn't, so we took off our skates. The party wasn't over, but we didn't care. Anyway, half the fun of ice-skating is going back to normal, when stepping flat-footed onto the carpet makes everything feel brand-new.

July

JULY WAS SO HUMID that my bangs clumped together in thick, heavy strands. Sandra said I had nothing to complain about, and she lifted her own bangs to reveal a crop of angry bumps.

"See?" she said. "At least you don't have zits." She leaned back on the steps and scowled at the driveway. "It's because of that stupid hat. I *hate* that hat. I can feel the oil building up every second it's on my head."

Sandra had a summer job at Baskin-Robbins, and she had to wear a pink-and-brown hat with a pom-pom on top. She was supposed to be there now, hat in place, but Mom hadn't returned from the dry cleaners to give her a ride.

"Where *is* she?" Sandra demanded. "Doesn't she know this is my life, pathetic as it is?"

"Well . . . at least you get to work with Bo," I said. "That's a good thing."

"Yeah, right. I get to work with Bo, who gets to see me looking like the Creature from the Black Lagoon. That's a good thing?" She stood up and scanned the road. "Where the hell is she?"

"Sandra!" She didn't normally use words like that, and I found myself half nervous and half thrilled when they popped out of her mouth.

"Oh, grow up," Sandra said.

Mom pulled into the driveway, and Sandra and I hurried to the car.

"You're late," Sandra griped, climbing into the front seat. She jerked her seat belt over her chest while I scooted into the back by Ty.

"Tell me about it," Mom said. "The girl at the dry cleaners couldn't find your father's shirts, and then at the bank, there was only one teller on duty. . . ." She listed her day's trials as she drove back into town, adding that she still had several errands to do and that she'd never get them finished with me and Ty in tow.

"So, here, Winnie," she finished, reaching over the seat and handing me seven dollars. "I know I told you we'd go shoe shopping, but we're going to have to put it off until tomorrow. How about if you and Ty get some ice cream instead?"

"What?" Sandra cried. "You're leaving them with me?"

I grinned and stuffed the money in my pocket. Hanging out at Baskin-Robbins was far better than going shoe shopping. New sandals could wait until another day.

"Mom," Sandra said. "You can't expect me to baby-sit them while I'm at my job!"

"Hey, I don't need baby-sitting," I said. "Anyway, *I'll* be the one baby-sitting Ty. Right, Mom?"

Sandra tried using her patient voice. "Take them back home. Please, Mom."

Mom turned left into the strip mall, where Baskin-Robbins sat nestled between Joe May Cleaners and Jalisco's Mexican Restaurant. "I'm sorry, Sandra, but there's no time. We're already running late, remember?"

Sandra got out of the car. She glared at me through the window.

"Chocolate chip mint," Ty said, struggling to get out of his booster seat. "Okay, Winnie? With three cherries."

Bo has lean, brown arms and blond hair that sticks up in tufts around the brim of his hat. He's the pitcher for his high-school baseball team, and he was working at Baskin-Robbins to build up the muscle on his left forearm. He loved it when people ordered French Vanilla or Rocky Road, the two hardest ice creams to scoop, and if someone ordered a hand-packed pint of any flavor, he was in heaven. "Like a rock," I once heard him mutter as he packed a pint of Swiss Dark Chocolate. "Roy McCallum, prepare to meet your doom."

From the pink vinyl booth where I sat with my scoop of Rocky Road, I could study Bo to my heart's content. I watched him turn away from the soda machine, and it occurred to me that Bo is probably the cutest boy I've ever seen. Not probably: definitely. And not for the first time I wished I were sixteen instead of eleven so that Bo would grin at me like he grinned at Sandra after slipping an ice cube down her shirt to make her shriek.

I lifted a spoon of ice cream to my mouth. If Bo is the cutest boy in the world, which he is, then that makes Sandra the luckiest girl. Sandra, my sister, with her oily bangs and crop of zits. Also with her light blue eyes that look like water, and her smile that opens like a present when she's in a good mood.

"Is there a problem?" she asked me now, pausing with the scooper in one hand and an empty cone in the other.

"Huh?" I said.

"Quit staring. This isn't the WB, you know."

I went back to my ice cream, picking out the marshmallows and slivers of nut and putting them on a napkin. "Want these?" I asked Ty.

He dumped them on top of his chocolate-chip mint, then lifted his head and smiled. Like me, Ty has brown eyes and straight, brown hair. Boring, boring brown, like mud.

When we'd finished our scoops and all that was left were sticky droplets on the edges of our cups, I threw away our trash and marched Ty to the counter for round two. "Do you know what you want?" I prodded. I assumed my most adult expression and said to Bo, "He's so wishy-washy. When it comes to ice cream, I'm afraid he lacks a certain resolve."

Lacks a certain resolve was a phrase I'd picked up from Mom, who used it a couple of days ago to describe my aunt Lucy. Aunt Lucy had been studying to be a teacher, but she dropped out of her program and was now thinking about becoming a veterinarian.

Sandra stared at me as if I were crazy. "What?" she said. "He does not."

"Chocolate-Chip Mint," Ty announced.

"Are you sure?" I asked. "What about French Vanilla? Or Peanut Butter 'n Chocolate. You love Peanut Butter 'n Chocolate."

Ty stood on his toes to make himself taller. "Chocolate-Chip Mint. And three cherries."

"What about you?" Sandra said while Bo fixed Ty's cup. She put one hand on her hip.

"I'll wait for Bo," I said.

"Bo's busy."

"Well, I'm not sure yet."

"Well, decide."

The bell on the door jingled, and two guys strolled in, friends of Bo's. Sandra's cheeks turned red. "Come on, Winnie. Now or never."

Bo dropped the final cherry onto Ty's ice cream and slid the cup across the counter. "Here you go, buddy. Enjoy." He crossed the store to his friends. "Hey, guys! What's up?"

Sandra was still waiting, eyebrows lifted in sharp peaks.

"French Vanilla," I said.

She scowled. Unlike Bo, she hated scooping French Vanilla. "Pick something else."

"French Vanilla," I said stubbornly. "And don't skimp."

I hung out by the counter while I ate my ice cream, pretending to admire the cakes in the display case so Sandra would leave me alone. As soon as Bo's friends left, I edged over to where he was working. "Those are cute," I said, peering at the ice-cream-scoop clowns he was making. He topped each scoop with an upside-down cone, then used icing to add two eyes, a nose, and a mouth.

He grinned at me. "You like them?"

"Uh-huh." I squinted at the scoop he was working on. "You should give him eyebrows."

"Yeah?" He added two upside-down *V*s and stepped back to admire the effect. "Hey, Sandra, I think I might have found my calling."

Sandra punched in the drawer to the cash register and joined Bo at the worktable. "Is that one supposed to look psychotic?" she asked, pointing at a scoop of vanilla with uneven eyes. She turned to me. "Bo's busy, Winnie. Quit bothering him."

"I'm not bothering him. Anyway, it's a free country."

"For some of us," Sandra said under her breath.

I leaned forward on the counter. "So, how's the arm?" I asked Bo. I liked saying "the arm." It made me feel tough.

"The arm is spectacular," Bo said. He leaned over the counter and flexed. "Want to feel?"

I touched the curve of his muscle, which was hard and warm. I blushed and drew back my hand.

"Sandra?" Bo said, sticking his arm in front of her.

Sandra busied herself with wiping the counter. "I have no desire to touch 'the arm,' thank you very much."

"Oh, come on," Bo said.

"Touch the arm," I urged. "Do it, Sandra."

Ty slid out of the booth and came over to us. "What's going on?"

"Your sister doesn't want to touch the arm," Bo said. He made his face look very sad.

Ty turned to Sandra. His expression was worried. "Sandra!"

"Oh, all right," Sandra said. She poked Bo's arm.

"She touched the arm!" Bo cried.

Ty and I cheered.

Bo leaned over to give me a high five, and I held my hand extra stiff so there'd be a good slap. Sandra stared at us as if we were crazy, but inside she was smiling. Bo knew it, and so did I.

Outside the store, a horn honked.

"Mom's here," Sandra said.

I glanced through the window and saw Mom's station wagon. "No fair, she's early!"

"Thank God for small miracles. Go on, she's waiting."

Ty ran ahead while I lingered by the counter. "Maybe I could run out and ask—"

"No."

"But—"

"Winnie, go."

I turned to Bo, pleading with my eyes.

"Hey, she's the boss," Bo said. He stepped closer to Sandra and rubbed her neck. She didn't pull away.

Sometimes summer can last too long, especially if your best friend and your second-best friend are out of town at the exact same time and your sister has a job and all your little brother wants to do is microwave marshmallows and watch them swell into white, fluffy pillows.

"Why can't we rent a beach house?" I asked Mom. "Please?" Amanda's family had gone to Pawley's Island for an entire month, and all I could think about was how much fun she must be having. Amanda promised she'd bring me some shells or a sand dollar if she got lucky, but it wasn't enough. I wanted to be there myself. I wanted to rent a house next to Amanda's and have bonfires in the evenings and gaze at the stars.

"Winnie," Mom said, in that warning tone of I've-answered-that-question-enough.

"Okay, fine," I said. "But can't we do *something?* Go to Disney World or something?"

She put down her dishrag. "Honey, your dad and I would

love to go on a family vacation, but we can't just pick up and—"

"Just send me, then. I can take care of myself. Chantelle's visiting her grandparents in Tennessee, all by herself with just her cousins, and last year her granddad took them to the biggest water slide in the world."

Mom raised her eyebrows. "You want to stay with Grandmom Perry in Greensboro?"

I opened my mouth, then shut it. Grandmom Perry lives in a one-bedroom apartment that smells like Dentyne, and she goes to church on Wednesdays, Saturdays, and Sundays. Before every meal she makes me recite a Bible verse.

"I'll try to think of something, all right, Winnie?" Mom said. "Just . . . hold on."

I slumped lower in my chair. *Hold on,* while outside in the real world people rode waves and swooped down water slides and slipped ice cubes into one another's shirts. All I wanted was to join in.

"Stop it!" Sandra squealed. She struggled to escape Bo's grasp. "I swear to God, stop it!"

"Not until you say I'm king," Bo said. He straddled her on the sofa and tickled her her ribs. "Say it!"

"No way! You cheated!"

"Did not!"

"Did, too!"

I watched from the door to the den. Mom had taken Ty to a birthday party at World of Fun, and Sandra and Bo were supposed to be "including me in their plans," as Mom put it. But they were too busy including each other to even know I was there.

"Hey," I said. "What are you guys doing?"

Bo lifted his head. "Winnie, come help me tickle your sister."

"Don't you dare," Sandra said.

"What are you the king of?" I asked Bo.

"Everything."

"Oh, please," Sandra said.

He dug his thumbs into her sides, making her yelp. "But especially," he continued, "of doughnuts. I am and always will be King of Doughnuts, regardless of whether your sister has the strength of character to admit it." He finished with one last side tickle, then sat back and let Sandra up. "I ate ten. Your sister, a measly half dozen."

"Liar! I ate nine and you know it. And you ate nine, too, Bo Sanders." She looked at me, flushed and happy. "He ate half of the tenth and wadded the rest in his napkin."

"Krispy Kreme or Dunkin' Donuts?" I asked. Krispy Kreme doughnuts are so light that I'd once eaten an entire dozen by myself, which, if Bo and Sandra would take my word for it, made *me* the doughnut king.

"Dunkin' Donuts, of course," Bo said. "Who couldn't eat nine Krispy Kremes?"

"Enough," Sandra moaned, putting her hand on her stomach. "We have to stop talking about it."

"Oh, are you full?" Bo asked. He put his arm around Sandra's shoulders and made a tsking sound. "Poor thing. Didn't know your own limits, did you?"

Sandra let her head fall on his chest. "I'm begging you—shut up."

He laughed and tucked her hair behind her ears. I marveled at how comfortable they seemed with each other. Sandra, my sister, with a boy. Then I thought about how every day this week Sandra had stayed late at work, calling to say that Bo would drop her off after they took inventory or restocked the paper goods.

Sandra's eyes fell on me. "Don't you have something to do?"

"You're supposed to be hanging out with me," I said.

"You're eleven years old. You can hang out with yourself."

"But I'm bored."

"Well, go be bored somewhere else."

I leaned against the end of the sofa, not looking directly at either of them. "I can eat a raw egg," I said. This was not exactly true. However, once last year I had seen Alex Plotkin eat a raw egg, and I'd watched the guys around him cheer when he lifted his head and wiped his mouth.

"Big whup," Sandra replied.

"I could show you if you want."

Sandra looked exasperated. "Winnie—"

"No," Bo said. "This I want to see." He pushed himself up. "You want to do it here, or should we go to the kitchen?"

"Uh, kitchen. In case there's a mess."

"Like if you spew?" Sandra said.

But she let Bo pull her from the couch, and several minutes later the three of us sat around the kitchen table, Bo and Sandra at one end and me at the other.

"In case you spew," Sandra said again.

"She's not going to spew," Bo said. "Are you?"

I didn't answer. I held a glass in one hand and an egg in the other, its shell cool and smooth against my palm. I hesitated, then cracked the egg against the rim of the glass. The yolk squelched as it separated from the shell, and I grimaced. I'd forgotten how squelchy eggs were.

Little baby chick, said a voice inside me.

"Well?" Sandra said. "Are you going to do it, or are you going to wimp out?"

"I'm going to do it," I said. I just didn't know how. When Alex did it, did he do it all in one quick gulp? Or did he make the mistake of looking at it first: a wet, yellow eye in a pool of jelly?

"In this lifetime?" Sandra asked.

I raised the glass. The egg stared up at me.

"Ten," Bo said, "nine, eight—"

"Hey, wait a minute," I said.

"—seven, six, five, four—"

"No fair! You can't just—"

Sandra smirked and joined in. "Three, two . . . one!"

"Do it, Winnie!" Bo said.

"Now!" Sandra commanded.

I looked from Bo to Sandra to the egg, and then I screwed my eyes shut and tilted the glass, throwing my head back and forcing myself not to gag as the egg slipped, cold and oozy, over my tongue. I didn't even swallow. It shot down my throat before I had the chance.

"Yeah!" Bo cheered. "Way to go!"

"Wh-hoo," Sandra said. "You're amazing." She pushed back her chair and stood up. "Bo? You ready?"

"Huh?" he said. "Oh, right." He high-fived me on his way to the door. "You're a stud, Winnie. Never forget."

I scrambled out of my chair. "Hey! What are you doing? Where are you going?"

"It's four o'clock," Sandra said. "*Oprah*."

"Can I watch with you?" I asked, following them upstairs to Mom and Dad's room, where there was a second TV.

"No," Sandra said. "You can watch it in the den."

"I don't want to watch it in the den. The den's boring. I want to watch it with—"

Sandra pushed me away and shut the door. A second later came the click of the lock.

"But—" I stared at the door. Why was everything so hard sometimes? I was all alone and I had no friends and inside my stomach was a baby chick. Bo and Sandra had stuffed themselves with doughnuts. And me? I'd gotten stuck with an oozy baby chick.

I saw the yolk quivering in the glass, and my stomach quaked.

"Oh, no," I whispered. "Oh, no, oh, no." I knocked on my parents' door. "I think I'm going to throw up!"

No response.

"I'm serious! I think I'm going to throw up!"

"Winnie, shut up!" Sandra called. "God!"

I vomited onto the carpet, a yellow puddle the size of my hand.

The doorknob clicked as Sandra unlocked it. "Jesus, Winnie, couldn't you at least have gotten to the bathroom?" She put her hands on her hips. Then she knelt beside me, careful to avoid the throw-up, and brushed my hair off my forehead. "Come on, let's get you cleaned up."

Afterward, the carpet scrubbed and my mouth rinsed out with Listerine, I sat between Sandra and Bo and watched the tail end of *Oprah*. The topic was "Hunks Who Dress Like Slobs," and Bo asked Sandra if she'd still go out with him if he wore the same pair of underwear for three weeks running.

"Don't be disgusting," Sandra said.

"Yeah," I added. "You don't want me to throw up again, do you?"

"Don't even say it," Sandra said, shooting me a harsher look than I'd expected.

During the next commercial, I leaned close to Sandra and spoke into her ear. "Sorry I was such a pain."

"Good," she said. "You should be." She pressed her lips together. "Just don't tell Mom."

"I won't."

I settled more comfortably on the bed, aware of Bo's arm behind me as he reached to rub Sandra's neck. I thought about his scooper's muscle. I almost asked to touch it, but I didn't.

August

B E SURE TO HELP OUT around the house," Mom said, fixing my tag so it didn't stick out of my shirt. "And be agreeable at mealtimes. If Theresa serves tuna fish, then you eat tuna fish. No asking for special foods."

"I *know*," I said. The Wilsons' Honda pulled into our driveway, and I slung my duffel bag over my shoulder. "Bye, Mom! Love you!"

"Love you, too," Mom said. "Don't forget to wear sunscreen!"

It was strange riding in the car with just Mr. Wilson. I nodded sympathetically as he griped about Old Hairball, the manager who'd scheduled the unexpected meeting that brought him back to Atlanta. But my heart wasn't in it. If it weren't for Old Hairball, then Mr. Wilson would still be lolling about in the ocean while I melted into a puddle in the hot August sun.

But now—the beach, the beach, the glorious beach!

"Yes!" I'd yelped when Amanda called long-distance to invite me, even though it meant a six-hour drive both ways and even though I'd only get to be there for a long weekend. I didn't care about any of that. I hadn't been to the beach since I was eight, and now I got to join Amanda for three whole days. We'd be sleek and sparkling mermaids, splashing in the waves.

"You're here!" Amanda squealed.

"I'm here!" I squealed back. "I'm really here!"

We hugged and jumped up and down, and then I grabbed my bag and followed her up the wooden steps. The house was on stilts so that a big storm couldn't wash it away, and we had to climb an outside staircase to get to the main level.

"'Dave's Place?'" I said, reading the plaque on the door. It was decorated with shells and starfish. "Who's Dave?"

"The owner, I guess," Amanda said. "All the houses down here have names. Last year we stayed in Calico Cat, which was awesome because it actually had air-conditioning. But Dave's Place is even better because we're right on the beach." She pushed open the squeaky screen door. "Come on, I'll show you around."

Inside the house were more shells. There were shells on top of the TV, shells in little glass bowls, even shells on the walls, glued to a real fishing net that was strung above one of the sofas. Standing at the sink was Mrs. Wilson, who wiped her hands on a dishcloth and came over to give me a hug.

"Winnie, we're so glad you could come," she said. "How was the ride?"

"Fine," I said. "Thank you so much for inviting me."

"Our pleasure," Mrs. Wilson said. "I'll go help Ted unload. I told him to pick up a few things for this weekend."

Amanda pulled me toward the back of the house. "This is our room," she said, pointing to a room with green walls. The bed had a green bedspread on it, and three big conch shells sat on the dresser. "We can change in here, but we'll probably sleep out on the sofas. It gets stuffy during the night."

She gave me a quick tour of the bathroom, her parents' room, and the kitchen, then led me to the front porch. "And now for the most important thing of all."

We stepped outside. The stars were out, and a hundred yards away I saw white foam rolling into the shore. I breathed in the salty air.

"Come on!" Amanda said. She loped down the walkway. I thought she'd stop when she reached the end, but she leapt onto the beach and kept going.

"Wait!" I cried.

She turned around. "What?"

"It's dark out!"

"So?"

"So what if a crab bites me?"

She ran back and took my hand. "Goof," she said. "You

have to get in the ocean when you first get here. It's a rule."

"It is?"

I resisted for the first couple of steps, but then I kicked off my shoes and let Amanda pull me along. The sand squeaked as we ran. At the ocean's edge, we stopped and let the waves lick our feet.

"A teeny bit deeper," Amanda urged. "Nothing's going to bite you, I promise."

I eased in up to my shins, then up to my knees. A wave splashed my shorts, and I laughed.

"Isn't it wonderful?" Amanda asked.

My heart swelled with joy. Then something squirmed beneath my foot, and I shrieked and dashed for the shore.

The next morning, Amanda and I woke at dawn. At home, I sleep until nine-thirty or ten, but at home I don't hear waves crashing or seagulls crying outside my window. Plus, at home I have blinds. Here in the beach-house living room, the bright sun shot through the filmy curtains and made Amanda and me blink and squint.

We wolfed down a quick breakfast of Cap'n Crunch and milk, then slipped into our swimsuits. Amanda wore a new bikini—white with splashy purple flowers—and I felt dumpy and plain in last year's saggy one-piece. Even Amanda's mother commented on it, although I don't think she meant it the way it sounded. "We're going to have to spruce you up if you want to catch any boys," she teased, screwing the lid on a thermos of Crystal Light. "Amanda, what about your red bikini with the stripes? Wouldn't that look precious on Winnie?"

"That's okay," I said, because I could tell from Amanda's expression that she didn't want me borrowing it. I could understand. Bathing suits are tricky to share.

Outside, we shook out our towels and spread them on the sand. Amanda's was pink. Mine was kind of gray and had Donald Duck on it. We sat down and leaned back on our elbows.

"Ciggie, dahling?" Amanda asked, drawing a pretend cigarette to her mouth.

"Why, certainly," I drawled. "The craving has been unbearable." I took a drag of my own fake cigarette and collapsed into a spasm of coughs. "Ahhh"—cough, cough—"now that's the ticket. Wouldn't you say, dahling?"

Amanda poured me a cup of Crystal Light, which I drank in tiny, sophisticated sips even though I'd have rather had grape Kool-Aid. The Crystal Light had that sugar-free aftertaste that Amanda used to hate as much as I did, but I figured if Amanda could get used to it, so could I.

"Swish it around and then go like this," Amanda said, pulling back her lips and baring her teeth.

"Why?" I said.

"It'll bleach your teeth and make them really white."

I pulled back my lips and bared my teeth. I felt like a tiger. A man walking by raised his eyebrows, and I cracked up.

"You can't laugh. You'll ruin it," Amanda said.

"Oh, plop," I said. "Who cares?" I wedged my cup into the sand and flipped onto my stomach. A few yards in front of us was a little girl about Ty's age. She was inverting buckets of sand and decorating the domes with shells.

"Want to build a sand castle?" I asked Amanda.

"I need to work on my tan," she said. She closed her eyes. "Maybe in a while."

I rested my chin in my palms and gazed at the ocean. I loved how it changed every single second while at the same time remaining so solidly *there*. I could stare at it for hours—except sweat was pooling in the hollows behind my knees, and my bathing suit was creeping up my bottom. I stood up and tugged at the elastic.

"Be back in a bit," I told Amanda. She nodded drowsily.

I walked over to the little girl. "Hi," I said, squatting beside her. "I'm Winnie."

"I can't make this flag stay in," the girl said. She handed me a stick with a piece of seaweed wrapped around it. "Can you do it for me?"

"Sure." I pushed the stick into the highest ridge of her castle and watched the sand crumble around the top. "We need it to be wet," I pronounced. "Go get some wet sand in your bucket and bring it back."

"Okay." The girl trotted down to the water, and I arranged the seaweed to make it look more like a real flag. When she came back, we dripped clumps of sand around the stick's base.

"Ta-da!" I said.

"Now we need to build a moat," the girl said.

Before long, Eliza and I had constructed an entire sand village. (Her mom told me Eliza's name when she brought us both a Popsicle. "How nice you are to play with Eliza," she said to me. "Eliza, you'll be a big girl, too, one day. Can you believe it?") We were putting the finishing touches on our dungeon when Amanda strolled over. She had a red mark on her cheek from lying on her towel.

"What are you doing?" she asked.

"Making a sand trap for our dungeon," I told her. "If someone walks over this hole"—I demonstrated with my fingers—"then, aaaah! Down to the fiery furnace!"

"But only the bad people," Eliza said.

Amanda didn't look impressed. In fact, she looked a bit as if she thought it was dumb, which made me realize that maybe it was. She asked if I was ready to go swimming, and I said, "Sure," and got to my feet.

"See you," I told Eliza.

After splashing around for an hour or so, we dragged out the rubber inner tubes Amanda's dad had brought from home. We swam with them past the breaking waves, and

Amanda showed me how to heave myself in so that my bottom stuck through the inner tube's hole and my arms and legs draped over the sides. Then it was like drifting around in our own portable potties, although of course we didn't actually pee or anything. (Well, all right, I did. But only because I didn't want to trudge all the way back to the house after working so hard to get to the exact right spot in the water. Anyway, fish pee in the ocean, so what's the big deal?)

The one thing we had to watch out for were the valve stems, which were the little metal things that stuck out on the inside edge of the tubes. When Mr. Wilson filled the tires with air, that's where he attached the pump. In the water, I had to be careful how I sat, because if my thigh rubbed up against the valve stem, it really hurt. Also, I didn't want the valve stem too near my armpit, because then when I reached back to paddle, it scraped my side.

I was scooching myself into a better position when Amanda said, "Winnie, look! Quick, before it's too late!"

I swiveled my head. "What? Where?"

"There!" Amanda said. "Those two guys. See them?"

I breathed out. "Jeez, Amanda. I thought there was a shark or something." I sank back into the inner tube, although I didn't let my feet dangle quite so deep. "The guys standing by the water—are they the ones you're talking about?"

"The one in the red muscle shirt is *so* cute," Amanda said. "Don't you think? He's been here this whole week, but I haven't gotten the chance to talk to him."

I squinted. "His friend is scratching his . . . you know."

"Winnie!"

"Well, he is."

"That is just nasty," Amanda said. But she giggled, which made me feel good. "Come on, let's go over."

"Why?" I asked.

She giggled again. "What do you mean, *why?*" She back-stroked toward the boys.

My stomach tightened, but I paddled after her. The closer we got, the more nervous I felt. What were we supposed to say once we got there?

We squirmed off our inner tubes and lugged them to shore. By this time, Red Shirt and Nasty were ambling toward the pier.

"Hurry, they're getting away!" Amanda said. We chugged up the beach and dropped our inner tubes by our towels, then fast-walked back to the waterline, where the sand was harder packed. I felt sticky from salt, and the insides of my thighs rubbed together.

"I think I'm starting to burn," I said. "Maybe we should go back."

Amanda adjusted her bikini top. "Don't be silly."

We climbed the steps to the pier. At the shore end was a bait-and-tackle shop, and I looked longingly at the large cooler by the door. A Dr Pepper sounded wonderful. But Red Shirt and Nasty were heading out to watch the fisher-man, so that's what we did, too.

"We'll walk to the very end," Amanda said. "If they want to talk to us, they can. Do I look all right?"

I stared at her. Since when did she care how she looked? I glanced down at my own splotchy legs and worn bathing suit. "Do I?" I asked.

"Except for your hair," she said. She reached over and smoothed it down. "Okay, let's go."

She scampered down the pier, and I followed more slowly. Between the wooden planks were inch-wide gaps and the occasional rotted-out hole, and peering down, I saw first sand, then water. The farther out we got, the scarier it was. I knew I wouldn't fall through—the holes weren't *that* big— but the sight of the waves that far below made me dizzy.

Halfway down the pier, Amanda stopped. Red Shirt and Nasty were leaning against the railing and studying the ocean. Up close I saw that they were older than I'd thought, like sixteen or seventeen. Bo's age. Only Bo was sweet and kind and wonderful, while these guys were . . . hairy. At least, Nasty was. Tufts of dark hair sprouted from his armpits and curled on his legs. Red Shirt had armpit hair, too, although his was blond. They both wore board shorts low on their hips.

"Man," Red Shirt said.

Nasty whistled. "Wouldn't want to get stung by those babies."

Amanda sauntered over, deliberately looking at the water

and not at Red Shirt. Then her eyes bugged, and she said, "Oh my God."

"What?" I said.

"You've got to see this, Winnie. Oh my *God*."

I joined her at the railing. Below us was the ocean, lapping against the barnacle-crusted posts of the pier. And floating in the water—sheez, there must have been a hundred of them!—was a colony of green-and-blue jellyfish with transparent, bulging bodies.

I gripped the railing. My legs felt heavy.

"Can you see their tentacles?" Amanda asked.

I could when the water fanned them out. Slippery pale strands that were two to three feet long.

"They're filled with poison sacs," Amanda said. "If a fish brushes up against them, or a person, the poison can hurt so bad it paralyzes them. People have died from getting stung by jellyfish."

I shuddered. "Yikes."

"Uh-huh. A couple of summers ago I stepped on part of a dead jellyfish. A fisherman had reeled it up, and I guess one of its tentacles got smeared onto the pier. The bottom of my foot got all dimpled like I'd stepped on a jillion little suction cups, and I was, like, hopping around and screaming because it hurt so much."

"Can you imagine being in the water and getting tangled up in one?" I asked.

"Or swimming into a whole swarm of them and feeling their tentacles wrap around you?"

We gazed at the bobbing, iridescent mass. The jellyfish were actually kind of pretty from way up here.

"Hey," Amanda said, straightening up. "Where's Red Shirt?"

I glanced around.

"There, down at the end," she said. She headed toward him, then turned back when she realized I hadn't moved. She sighed. "Now what's the problem?"

"They're *old,*" I said, my heart thumping.

"So?"

"So . . . I don't know." Amanda didn't used to care about boys. Why had she suddenly gotten interested?

"Winnie. We're already here," she said. When I still hung back, she put her hands on her hips. "What, you'd rather build sand castles with your little friend?"

I felt a hot blush creep up the back of my neck. Tears stung my eyes.

Amanda looked away. In a tight voice, she said, "Well, I'm going over. You can do whatever you want."

I swallowed. I made my feet start moving and followed a yard behind her, swiping at my eyes.

"Hey," Amanda said to Red Shirt's back. He and Nasty were gazing out over the end of the pier, but they turned at her voice.

"Hey yourself," Red Shirt said. He looked her over.

"Are you, like, a surfer?" she asked. "I saw you surfing the other day, and you were really good."

Red Shirt glanced at Nasty. I could tell he was amused. He propped his weight on his elbows and said, "We do a little surfing, yeah. Are *you* a surfer?"

"Ha," Amanda said. "I wish. It would be so cool to know how to do that. Don't you think, Winnie?"

I stared at the floorboards. "Uh-huh."

"Maybe we should teach you," Nasty said, winking at Red Shirt. "Give you your own private lessons. What do you think?"

"Yeah!" Amanda said. "That would be awesome!"

Nasty and Red Shirt laughed. Nasty held out his palm, and Red Shirt slapped him a high five.

"I'm *serious*," Amanda said. "I'm a really fast learner, I swear!"

This made Nasty hoot. I wrapped my arms around my ribs and wanted to disappear.

Red Shirt grinned. "Find me in five years, babydoll." He tweaked her nose. "Come on, bro. Let's bounce."

Amanda watched them go. She was pink with pleasure. "He called me 'babydoll,'" she whispered.

I exhaled, grateful for the narrow escape.

That night, things between Amanda and me were weird, only she pretended they weren't, which made it even worse. At dinner, Mrs. Wilson asked if we'd had a good day, and

Amanda said, "Oh my God, we had a *super* day. Didn't we, Winnie? Mom, you should see this one shell Winnie found. It's pale orange with darker orange stripes, and it's soooo pretty."

I couldn't figure out why she was acting so dumb. First all mean at the pier—because it *was* mean, what she said about me going to play with Eliza—and now all la-di-da like nothing had happened. But to tell the truth, I didn't want to figure it out. I just wanted us to have fun like we always did.

We went for a starlit walk on the beach with her parents, which was tolerable because they did all the talking. After that, we washed up and got settled on our sofas. My sheets smelled like mildew. For several minutes we lay quietly, then through the dark came Amanda's voice.

"Do you think Red Shirt likes me?" she asked. She spoke softly, so her parents wouldn't hear from their bedroom. "It was so sweet how he asked if I was a surfer. I think that was a good sign, don't you?"

I made a noise that could have meant anything.

"And Nasty obviously likes you," she went on. "He talked to you and everything. So you can have him, and I'll take Red Shirt, okay?"

I shifted on the lumpy sofa. I didn't want either of them. And I didn't want them here between us, hovering in the salty air. "Those jellyfish were really creepy," I finally said.

"Tell me about it," Amanda said.

"Just think: They're out there right this second, floating and bobbing along."

Amanda made a shivery sound. "Sharks, too, smelling the water for blood. Oh my God, I would totally freak if I ever saw a shark."

"I heard of this boy once who got his leg chomped off by a shark," I said. "He had to swim back to shore with nothing but a bloody stump."

"Ew!" Amanda said. "That is so scary!"

We imagined being trapped at sea with only an old plank to hold on to, and how terrifying that would be. Or what if we were caught in a hurricane with twenty-foot waves? Then we branched out to include other natural disasters, like tidal waves, floods, tornadoes.

I warned Amanda that if she was ever on the highway when a tornado came, she should climb under an overpass and press up against one of the concrete support thingies. I'd seen a special on the Weather Channel about tornadoes, and a man had kept his children safe by doing exactly that. I drifted into a fantasy where I was caught in a tornado, me and this one little girl who'd gotten separated from her mom, and I dragged her under the overpass and zipped my jacket around her to prevent her from blowing off.

I don't know how much of this I had explained out loud and how much had stayed in my head when Amanda next spoke.

"Giant squid," she whispered. "Squelching along where you can't even see them."

"Ooo, good one," I whispered back. I pulled my sheet up under my chin, and the drone of the waves lulled me to sleep.

Saturday was our last full day. The sky was cloudy, and Amanda was pissed.

"Why can't it be cloudy tomorrow?" she complained. "This is my final chance to work on my tan!"

"You still get sun when it's overcast," her mother reminded her. "You actually get more, because the sun's rays reflect off the clouds."

"Yeah, but it doesn't *feel* the same." She scowled and scooped her inner tube from the porch. "Come on, Winnie. We might as well go in the water."

The ocean was warmer than the air, and after swaying up and down in the waves for a while, Amanda perked up.

"I love it here so much," she said. "When I'm grown up, I'm going to have my very own beach house, and not just for a month every summer, but for whenever I want."

"That would be so awesome," I said. Things felt okay between us, and I swirled my fingers in the water. "Hey, I've got a great idea. Let's buy one together and call it Winanda's Hideaway."

"'Winanda'?" Amanda said.

"It's our names combined," I explained.

She laughed and rolled her eyes like she thought I was kidding. The sun eased out from behind a cloud, and she tilted her face toward the sky. *"Yes,"* she said. She spread her hair over the inner tube. "I should have put lemon juice in. I want to go to school with streaky, sun-kissed hair. We start in two weeks, can you believe it?"

"We better be in the same homeroom," I said.

"I *know,*" Amanda said. "If we're not, I'll die. Hey, can you fix my strap for me?" She leaned forward, and I stretched sideways and straightened her strap. Beyond her, I could see the pier.

"We are really far out," I said, gauging the distance by the pier posts.

Amanda turned curiously. "Wow," she said. "We are."

Something occurred to me, and I frowned. "Isn't this how far out we were when we saw the jellyfish?"

Together, we looked down.

"Crap!" Amanda cried. She started backstroking. "They're everywhere!"

They *were* everywhere—pale, shimmering blobs floating all around us. Fear zinged my spine, and I drew in my arms and legs and tried to hitch my bottom out of the water. My elbow brushed against something gelatinous, and I screamed.

"Paddle, Winnie!" Amanda ordered.

"I can't! What if I touch one?!"

"You have to! Just keep your arms up high!" She was already several yards away from me.

I kept my elbows close to my sides and paddled, using only my hands to flap at the water. I got nowhere. A wave swelled under me, then lifted Amanda's inner tube and carried it twenty feet in.

"Wait for me!" I yelled.

"Win*nie!*" Amanda called.

My pulse raced. I could hardly breathe. I screwed up my face and backstroked, and my entire body recoiled when I touched another jellyfish. I craned my neck and saw Amanda almost at the shore.

"You can do it!" she yelled. She clambered off her inner tube in knee-deep water.

I backstroked again. Then again. Each time a wave came, my heart leapt into my throat. I was terrified that a jellyfish would wash into my lap. *Go, go, go,* I told myself.

"You're almost there!" Amanda cried. "Don't stop!"

Stroke by stroke, I struggled toward the shore. The jellyfish thinned out, and the waves got more lively, crashing into white foam before rolling back to the sea. A two-footer broke on top of me, and I flipped off my inner tube and was dragged against sand. I stumbled to my feet and churned through the receding water, then dropped down on the beach.

Amanda bolted over. "Winnie, are you okay?" She clutched my hand. "Can you talk? Are you in shock? Were you stung?"

"I'm fine," I said, although my teeth were chattering. "But I left my inner tube. I'll go get it in a minute."

"You think I care about the inner tube?" she asked. "Cripes, Winnie, I thought you were a goner!"

"Me, too," I said.

We looked at each other, and then we got the giggles.

"All those jellyfish—".

"Hundreds of them!"

"And then that wave came, and I was like, 'Bye, Amanda!'"

"And I was like, 'Bye, Winnie!' Only I didn't *mean* to leave you. It just happened!"

People were staring, but we couldn't stop laughing. A snot bubble ballooned from one nostril, and I wiped my nose with the back of my hand. Several yards away I caught sight of someone familiar.

"Great," I said. "Look who's here." It was Red Shirt and Nasty, regarding us as if we belonged back in kindergarten. I tried to pull myself together. I tried to act mature. "You want to go talk to them? Because you can if you want."

Amanda glanced up. Her fingers flew to the strap of her bikini. Then she pressed her lips together and said, "Oh, please. With my best friend stranded helpless on the beach?"

That threw us into chortling snort-laughs, and we collapsed backward on the sand.

September

EVERYONE SAYS CHANGE is what makes life an adventure. That when you change, you grow, and if you don't change, you'll shrivel up and rot like an old potato.

Well, baloney. The people who get rah-rah over change are always parents and librarians, not kids. Because when kids change, it's really pretty ugly. Three times out of four it means someone's going to get her feelings hurt, or someone's going to feel stupid when the day before she felt just fine. Three times out of four it means someone's two best friends are out of the blue going to start acting silly and giggly and full of secret looks, and nothing that someone can do will make things go back to normal.

It makes me want to cry.

After all, it wasn't my fault I did a giant cannonball at Chantelle's neighborhood pool and drenched Amanda and Chantelle from head to toe. How was I supposed to know they wanted to stay dry and perfect for the too-tan lifeguard with the squinty eyes? We were at a *pool*. You're *supposed* to get wet.

And so what if Amanda and Chantelle both shaved their

legs for the very first time the week before school started? Big whup. That didn't mean they had to call me "prickle puss" for five days running, touching my legs and then jerking back like they'd been poked by a needle. Even if they were joking, it wasn't a nice thing to do.

Maybe Amanda had been changing already. Maybe it started at the beach, or even earlier. But it wouldn't have been such a problem—I know for a fact—if Gail Grayson hadn't prissed onto the scene. Well for all I cared, good ol' Gail could march right out of Ms. Russell's sixth-grade class in her lemon-colored skirt and matching tights. Even if I knew I'd never see her again, I wouldn't shed a tear. Amanda and Chantelle would beg her to stay, but not me. Although I might go to the office the next day and ask very politely if I could change classes, since if Gail left, Ms. Russell would have an extra space. Mr. Hutchinson wouldn't care, and then I'd be back with Amanda where I belonged.

"And another thing," Gail said, interrupting my thoughts and bringing me back to the playground. She glanced at the girls doing gymnastic moves on the basketball court, then back at us. "If we're going to be in a club together, it's important we look our best. We shouldn't just wear shorts and T-shirts, and we should take some time doing our hair. Like, if we have bangs, we should curl them with a curling iron, just as an example." She looked at me. "I could show you how, if you want."

I glared. She could curl her bangs all she wanted, but mine were staying nice and straight, thank you very much. And what was wrong with my Atlanta Braves T-shirt? I liked how big it was, and how the lettering across the front had cracked from being washed so many times. Most of all, I liked the fact that I wasn't being all fancy and frilly just because it was the first day of school. Unlike some people I know.

Gail blushed the tiniest amount. "I mean, not that they look bad the way you've got them. It's just that in Chicago, it's, like, a crime not to look the best you possibly can."

"If Chicago's so great, then why aren't you there?" I asked.

"Winnie!" Amanda said.

Gail turned even redder, but she lifted her chin and said, "Look. No one said you had to join our club. Maybe it should only be for people in Ms. Russell's class. And for your information, my father got a promotion, but my mom says it's too hot here and she wishes we'd just move back."

"She's not the only one," I muttered.

"So are you in or not?" Gail said.

I looked at Amanda. I looked at Chantelle. I looked across the playground at the girls doing gymnastics. Louise, who'd been to gymnastics camp, was showing the others how to do a back walkover, while Karen tried to balance on her hands but couldn't get her feet to stay up. Both wore matching pink T-shirts and overalls. Five yards away, Dinah Devine sat alone on the concrete steps. Dinah, wouldn't you know it, was in Mr. Hutchinson's class with me. This morning when she saw me, she smiled and called, "Winnie, over here! I saved you a seat!"

"Oh, Winnie, just do it," Amanda said. "It won't be any fun without you."

"Anyway, you have to help us pick out a name," Chantelle said. "We can't have a club without a name."

I shrugged. "Fine, I'll be in your stupid club."

Gail's eyes flicked over me, but I couldn't tell what she was thinking.

The next morning, I dug out Mom's curling iron from the bottom drawer in her bathroom and plugged it in, just as an experiment. I'd worn my hair the same way ever since I could remember, and maybe it *was* time I tried something new. Not because Gail told me to. And if she said anything, I'd give her the evil eye.

But I'm in the sixth grade now. Next year I'd start junior high. I didn't want to be the one kid in school who looked like she belonged in day care.

Amanda and Chantelle have it easy. Amanda has thick, blond hair as shiny and straight as Alice in Wonderland's, and without even trying she always looks cute. She somehow knows to wear a purple headband with her yellow and white sundress, for instance. But if I try to mix and match, I end up looking like an oil spill. Plus, Amanda has freckles, which according to Robert Bond look like tiny hearts. I've wanted freckles forever, and I don't have a single one.

And Chantelle. In my opinion she's the prettiest girl in the sixth grade, far prettier than Gail. She has dark brown hair and dark brown eyes, and she's the only person I've ever met whose eyelashes curl up like the models in Amanda's *Seventeen*. Her skin is the color of Nestlé's Quik, and her teeth are straight and white. My teeth are a little crooked. Mom says I might need braces.

I touched the rod of Mom's curling iron and snapped back my hand. It was hotter than I'd expected. I picked up the handle, getting a feel for how the clamp opened and closed. It didn't seem hard. If I was going to use it, though, I needed to go ahead and get started. This morning the three sixth-grade classes were meeting to talk about school pictures, and Amanda had promised to sit with me.

I raised the curling iron and clamped down on a chunk of my bangs. I counted to ten, then carefully released the handle. Not bad. The bangs on the right side of my face now curved under in a smooth arc, like the cap of a mushroom.

I looked at my watch—7:20. Usually I'd be heading out the door by now, but I couldn't go with my bangs half done. Although it would be funny. "In Atlanta, all the girls wear their bangs like this," I'd tell Gail. "In Atlanta, it's, like, a crime to look totally froufrou every minute of your life."

I clamped the left side of my bangs and started counting.

"Winnie!" Mom called. "Time for school!"

I didn't answer. Eight more seconds.

"I'll get her," I heard Ty say. His footsteps pounded down the hall. "Hey, Winnie! Mom says—"

"Wait! Don't come in!" I leaned toward the mirror and squeezed the handle.

"—or you'll be late and she's *not* going to drive you!" He barreled into the bathroom, ramming into my legs and knocking me forward.

"Ow!" I bellowed as the rod touched my skin. "Ow, ow, ow!"

The curling iron clattered to the counter. I grabbed a washcloth, stuck it under the faucet, and jammed it against my forehead. I pulled it away, revealing an angry red burn that was already turning blistery. "Great, Ty! Thanks a lot!"

Mom appeared at the door of the bathroom. She took in the scene, then stepped closer and gently pushed back my bangs. "Ouch," she said.

"It kills," I whined. I twisted away from her and stared at my reflection. Even with my bangs hanging normally, you could still see the burn. "There's no way I'm going to school."

"Oh, I think you better," Mom said.

"But everyone will see!"

"Do you want me to put on a Band-Aid?"

The only Band-Aids in the cabinet had Barney on them. I begged Mom with my eyes.

"I'm sorry you burned yourself, Winnie, and I'm sorry it hurts. But you're not staying home. Now scoot downstairs and get moving."

By the time I got to school, the gym was packed. Mrs. Jacobs held up her hands, but no one paid attention. "Students," she said into the microphone. "Students, please!"

"Take a seat, Winnie," Mr. Hutchinson said. He saw my forehead and his eyebrows shot up. "What happened to you?"

I scanned the floor, looking for the empty spot that would help me find Amanda. "I kind of had an accident."

"I'll say. Do you need a Band-Aid?"

I craned my neck, still searching.

"Well, go on and sit down," he said. "Mrs. Jacobs is trying to start."

"I will. I'm just looking for—"

He took my shoulders and guided me to the last row of students, right next to Dinah Devine. "Sit."

"Winnie! Hi!" Dinah said, lighting up as if I'd sat there on purpose. She beamed and launched in about teachers and classes and how exciting it was to be a sixth grader at last. Then she fished around in her backpack, saying something about her sticker collection and how she'd been working on it all summer.

"Want to see?" she asked. "I know it's here somewhere."

I tuned her out, because four rows up I finally spotted Amanda. To her left sat Chantelle and to her right sat Gail, with no space between them at all. My heart lurched.

Dinah plopped a spiral notebook into my lap and turned to a page full of kittens. "These are my favorites. You can have one if you want." She looked up and sucked in a breath of air. "Ooo. What happened to your head?"

Ahead of me, Gail cupped her hand over Amanda's ear and whispered something secret. Amanda whispered something back, and the two of them laughed.

"Shh," I said to Dinah. I got a stinging feeling in the back of my throat, and I dug my fingernails into my palms. "We're not supposed to talk."

For the rest of the day, I avoided Amanda. She obviously didn't need me, so why should I need her? Only, I did. Lunch was boring without her to crack jokes with, and staying inside during recess made me feel like a loser. Mr. Hutchinson offered to let me feed Hannibal, the sixth-grade class snake, but I turned him down. Somehow I doubted that dropping a dead mouse into a corn snake's gaping mouth would make me feel better.

At home, I went straight to my room, and when the phone rang, I almost didn't answer. I didn't *want* to answer—I had better things to do than talk to people who didn't even save me a seat—but my hand betrayed me. When I heard Amanda's voice, my stomach got shaky.

"Where were you all day?" she asked. "I know you weren't absent, because Dinah asked me during recess if I knew how you burned your forehead. Are you okay?"

"I'm fine," I said.

"Well, what happened? Dinah acted like it was this big deal that she knew something about you that I didn't."

"Nothing happened. I burned myself with the curling iron. It was no big deal. And the only reason Dinah knew was because Mr. Hutchinson made me sit next to her in assembly." I clutched the phone. "Why didn't you save me a seat?"

"I *did* save you a seat, but you never came! And finally Ms. Russell made Chantelle scoot over so more people could squeeze in."

I bit my lip. If Chantelle had to scoot over, then the space Amanda saved was between the two of them. Which meant that Gail would have sat next to Amanda either way.

I guess Amanda figured out that I wasn't going to respond, because she said, "*Anyway,* we finally came up with a name for our club."

"Oh, yeah? What?"

"The Aqua Girls."

"The *Aqua* Girls?"

"I think it sounds sophisticated," she said. "Like we're glamorous dancers or something."

"Where, at Sea World? Amanda, that is the dumbest name I've ever heard."

She exhaled. "Well, if you'd have been there, you could have—"

"Who picked it out? Gail?"

"We all did. Gail thought of it first, but we all agreed."

I shook my head. "That is absolutely the dumbest name I've ever heard."

For a few seconds we sat there breathing, and I worried I'd gone too far. In my mind I saw Amanda and Gail during assembly, how their shoulders touched when they leaned together.

I cleared my throat. "Amanda—"

"The thing is, tomorrow's picture day," she said before I could finish. Her voice was cooler than before. "We thought it would be a good idea if we all wore the same-color shirts."

"What, like Karen and Louise?"

Amanda was silent. Then she said, "If you don't want to, Winnie—"

"No, I want to. I was kidding." I closed my eyes. "So, um, what color?"

"Turquoise."

"*Turquoise?*"

"Winnie—"

"Great. Fabulous. I love turquoise."

Amanda sighed. "I've got to go. I'll see you tomorrow."

"Sure," I said. "Tomorrow."

That night, I couldn't fall asleep no matter how hard I tried. First was the issue of the turquoise shirt. I didn't own a turquoise shirt. I didn't own anything turquoise, period. I had a midnight-blue T-shirt that I loved, as well as a light blue button-down that used to be Sandra's. But neither counted as turquoise, and I didn't want Gail gazing at me with her lizard eyes as if I were too dumb to know the difference. Mom had a turquoise shirt, but it had long, flowing sleeves and a floppy bow above the top button. When I asked if I could borrow it, she wanted to know what kind of costume I was putting together.

"Is it for a play?" she had said.

"It's not for a play. It's just to wear. So can I?"

She fingered the shirt's bow and squelched a grin. "Sure, Winnie, if you want to. You know, this blouse used to belong to your grandmom Perry. She wore it every Sunday for ten years, back when she played the piano for her church choir."

I grabbed the shirt and stomped out of the room.

The second reason I couldn't fall asleep was because I couldn't stop thinking about Amanda and Gail. What if Amanda decided to be Gail's best friend instead of mine? I thought about Sandra and Angie Newsom. What if Amanda *outgrew* me, like Sandra outgrew Angie? I'd still have Chantelle, but Chantelle has about a dozen cousins she saw every weekend, and one of them, Darlene, is in sixth grade the same as us. She doesn't go to our school, but she and Chantelle are really close. There isn't room between them for me.

When Amanda and I were seven, we pricked our fingers with a needle and pressed them together, mixing our blood. Where was Gail then, huh? And why didn't she stay there, where she belonged?

But the biggest reason I couldn't fall asleep was because my forehead still hurt where I'd burned it with the curling iron. If I lay on my side like I normally did, my pillow pressed into the burn and made it ache. I tried lying on my back, but that didn't work either because I never slept that way. Finally, I curled up on my side and twisted my neck as far as I could in the opposite direction so that my forehead didn't touch my pillow. It wasn't very comfortable, but gradually my thoughts grew muddled and I slipped into a troubled sleep.

I woke up the next morning with Sweetie-Pie snuggled against my side. The song playing on my radio alarm was one I liked, and even Grandmom Perry's turquoise shirt, which I'd draped over the top of a chair, didn't look quite as hideous as I'd originally thought. A warm coziness seeped through me, and for a moment I couldn't even remember why I'd been so worried the night before. I mean, I *remem-*

bered, but none of it seemed quite so important anymore. Amanda was probably just being nice to Gail since Gail was new. I could be nice to her, too. We could be nice to her together. Secretly we'd feel sorry for her, but we'd only let on when it was the two of us alone.

I sat up, and pain shot through my neck. I gasped and held still. Slowly, I moved my head, and the pain flamed up even worse. I tried turning my neck more gently, but it didn't help. I tried massaging it, but that didn't help either. I must have slept all night with my neck wrenched to the left, and now it was stuck that way.

I eased off the bed and took tiny, clockwise steps until I could see myself in the mirror. My heart stopped. With my head twisted to the side, I looked like a human flamingo. And today was school picture day, which meant that unless the photographer had everyone try an over-the-shoulder glamour shot, I was in big trouble. But I had to be there, because otherwise there'd be three Aqua Girls instead of four, and *I'd* be the one everyone felt sorry for, not Gail.

Tears welled in my eyes. Why did everything have to happen to me? Why couldn't I be normal like everyone else?

Stop it, I told myself. *Just stop it.* Maybe my neck muscles would loosen up between now and the time I got to school, and maybe by homeroom I'd be able to face forward. If not by homeroom, then surely by the time we got our pictures taken. Either way, crying would only make things worse. I had enough problems without adding puffy eyes to the list.

I carefully got dressed and grabbed my backpack, wincing each time I jarred my neck. "Bye!" I yelled, slipping through the front door while Mom was busy with Ty. Pain bloomed above my spine, but I made myself keep going.

In homeroom, the girls fidgeted with their hair and passed around compact mirrors while Mr. Hutchinson tried to read the announcements.

"Do my bangs look okay?" Karen asked. "Do you swear?"

"I told my mom I wanted to wear lipstick, but she wouldn't let me!" said Maxine.

Beside me, Dinah tightened the ribbon around her ponytail. "My picture always turns out horrible." She giggled and tugged at the waist of her dress. "I close my eyes every time. I can't help it."

"Just blink a lot before it's your turn," I said. My neck was still stuck, but I was trying to act casual. "That way your eyes will stay wet."

"Oh," she said. "Okay, I will." She glanced at me, then followed my gaze out the window. "What are you looking at?"

"Nothing," I said. I shifted sideways in my seat.

"Yes, you are. What is it? What's out there?"

"Class," Mr. Hutchinson said. "I've told you twice now. We need to walk quietly to the gym, where we'll join the other two classes for the sixth-grade group photo. Individual pictures will be taken row by row immediately afterward, so stay in place until your name is called. Does everyone understand?"

The girls squealed and hurried to the door, while the boys joked around and shoved each other out of place.

"Just tell me, Winnie," Dinah whispered. Even in the hall, she kept craning her neck to look where I was looking. "Are you pretending to be a spy?"

I walked faster and hoped no one else was watching.

"Winnie!" Amanda called when we reached the gym. "Over here!"

I could see her out of the corner of my eye, a shiny, turquoise blob standing next to two other turquoise blobs. I climbed the riser and edged in between Amanda and Gail.

"Good," Amanda said, "you wore turquoise." She paused. "Is that new?"

"Kind of," I said. I should have stood on Amanda's left side, I realized, so I could look at her while we talked. With her on my right, I had to twist my body almost all the way around in order to even see her.

I could feel Gail's eyes boring into the back of my head. "What's wrong with your neck?" she asked.

"Nothing," I said.

"Amanda," Gail said in a complaining kind of way, and I got the uneasy feeling that they had talked about me last night, just as Amanda and I had talked about Gail. Which was unfair, because even if I wanted to start fresh with Gail, Gail wasn't letting me.

Amanda bit her lip. "You're not . . . trying to be funny or something, are you?"

"I'm not trying to be anything!" I said.

"All right, kids," the photographer called. "On the count of three. One, two—" She broke off, straightening up from the camera with a frown. "Excuse me. You in the turquoise? I need you to face forward."

I rotated my body as best I could.

"All the way, please."

I turned so that my shoulders were even with everyone else's, only now my head faced Gail instead of the lens.

Gail pressed her lips together. "Stop it!" she said.

"Winnie?" Mr. Hutchinson said. He walked to the end of our row. "What's going on?"

"I can't," I whispered.

"Can't what?"

"Move my neck. It's stuck." Tears burned in my eyes, and I blinked hard to keep them back.

"Mr. Hutchinson, she's faking," Gail said. "She's trying to be funny and she's ruining everything."

"Hold on now, Gail," Mr. Hutchinson said. He handed me a Kleenex from his pocket. "Has this ever happened before?"

"No."

"Well, it sounds like you've got a stiff muscle." He held out his hand and helped me step down from the risers. "Come on. Let's get you to the nurse."

I caught a glimpse of Dinah as we passed the front row. She lifted her hand halfway as if to wave, then changed her mind and gnawed on her thumbnail. Everyone else just stared.

"Okay, kids, eyes on me," the photographer said. "One, two, three—smile!"

The nurse called Mom, who called Dr. Harper at the Youth Clinic, who told us to come on in. While Dr. Harper examined my neck, she told me a story about a kid who got his tongue stuck in a bottle of Welch's grape juice.

"Finally I told him we'd just have to smash it," she said. "I asked the nurse to get a hammer, and his eyes about popped out of his head. He yanked his tongue right out of there, you better believe it!"

I stared at her. Or rather, at the wall past her left shoulder, since that was the way my neck was turned. Did she think that story would cheer me up? I like Welch's grape juice, and sometimes I pack a bottle in my school lunch. I could see it now: my tongue turning purple in the bottle while Gail Grayson tugged on the other end and called me a faker.

"Here," Dr. Harper said, scribbling a prescription and handing it to Mom. "Have her take one immediately, then again every six hours if the stiffness doesn't go away."

"Muscle relaxers?" Mom said.

"Half the normal adult dose. It won't hurt her, although it might make her a little wobbly." She helped me down from the table. "And you, Miss Winnie, need to stop worrying so much. It's worrying that makes your muscles tense up."

Great, I thought, already dreading the walk back through the waiting room. *How very helpful.*

We stopped by the drugstore on the way home, and the pharmacist gave me a cup of water so I could take my first capsule. By the time we got to the parking lot, I could barely keep my eyes open. Each time I put my foot down, I toppled sideways.

"What's wrong with her?" I heard a kid say as Mom helped me into the car. "Why can't she walk right?"

At home, Mom tucked me into bed and told me to call her if I needed anything. Just as I was drifting off, I heard the doorbell ring. I heard the squeak of the door, and then Mom's voice saying, "She's fine, Amanda, but I'm afraid she's resting right now. Why don't you—"

"I'm awake!" I called. I shook the fuzziness from my head. "Amanda! Up here!"

There was a pause as Mom said something I couldn't make out. Her heels clicked to the foot of the stairs and she called, "Five minutes, Winnie. That's all!"

Amanda jogged up the stairs and came into my room. She sat on the side of my bed. "Can you move your neck yet?" she asked.

"A little. Everything's blurry, though."

"Huh?"

"Your shirt." I giggled. "It looks like it's breathing."

Amanda looked at her chest.

My giggles petered out. I fooled with the edge of my sheet. "Gail thought I was faking, but I wasn't."

"I know."

"She's such a jerk." I said it like *of course,* like it was a fact that everyone knew, but under the covers my body felt sweaty. I checked Amanda's expression.

"Maybe," she finally said, "but she didn't mean to be. She thought you were making fun of her." She gnawed on her cheek, then let her breath out in a whoosh. "I can have more than one friend, you know."

My stomach did a flip-flop thing. "Yeah," I said. "Me and Chantelle."

"You know what I mean."

I didn't. For the millionth time today, I was afraid I was going to cry.

"So," she said, "will you be in school tomorrow?"

I shrugged.

"Well if you are, be sure to sit with me during lunch. Promise?"

"Will Gail be there?"

"Winnie . . ."

I closed my eyes. "My neck hurts pretty bad. The doctor said I should rest."

There was a pause, and then the bedsprings creaked as Amanda stood up. "We're in sixth grade now, Winnie. We can't just—"

"Okay," I said. "I mean, whatever. I'll see you tomorrow."

"At lunch?"

"Yeah. Sure. At lunch."

I squinted, watching her leave. Then I flopped my head back on my pillow, and everything went slippery around the edges. It didn't surprise me. Muscle relaxer or no muscle relaxer, sometimes the world is a big, fuzzy blur.

October

BY HALLOWEEN, the weather had grown chilly. Leaves scuttled across the road when the wind blew, and the air tingled as if something was burning. I looked outside, spooked by the thought of real witches flying to real hurly-burlies, then turned back to the miniature pizzas lined in neat rows before me. I pressed one black olive into the middle of each and brought the tray over for Mom to see.

"Eyeballs," I said.

"Beautiful," she said, taking the tray and sliding it into the oven. Along with the pizza eyeballs, I'd helped her make witch-brew punch, jack-o'-lantern sugar cookies with orange-and-black frosting, and, my own invention, smushed-brain vegetable dip. Mom suggested we call it something else for the sake of the guests, but I said no. Smushed-brain vegetable dip was perfect for Halloween.

Mom wiped her hands on her jeans and started cutting a block of Cheddar cheese into small cubes. "So have you thought any more about inviting Dinah?" she asked in a voice that was supposed to sound casual but didn't. "She could help you serve the hors d'oeuvres."

I got a tight feeling inside. I picked at a smudge on the counter and said, "Mom, no. I already told you."

"It's just that her father will be here, and—"

"What, Mr. Devine's going to fire Dad if Dinah isn't invited?"

"Of course not. But I hate to think of Dinah being alone on Halloween."

"Well, then maybe Mr. Devine should stay at home. He doesn't *have* to come to the party, you know."

Mom arched her eyebrows. But even though I felt a little bad, I didn't back down. I had planned on Amanda helping me pass around the hors d'oeuvres, not Dinah. We could have painted our faces green and told everyone we'd gotten food poisoning, then offered the platters of food and said, "You simply must try the cheese puffs. They're to die for."

But Amanda was going trick-or-treating with Gail at Gail's condominium complex. I could have gone, too, but I'd promised Mom I'd help with the party. Anyway, who wanted to see Gail prancing about in her blue satin princess costume with the gold-sequined crown?

Dinah is no princess, but she also isn't the type to paint her face green, and if I told her I had food poisoning, she'd probably believe me. Which might be fun for a while, but not for the whole night.

"Mom, Dinah's not . . . she's just not a Halloween-y kind of person. Besides, do I have to invite her to every single party in the world?"

Mom dumped the cubes of cheese into a plastic bowl and stuck the bowl in the microwave. "It's your decision, Winnie."

"Good. Then it's settled." Outside, a branch scraped the kitchen window, giving my spine a chill. "Hey, do you believe in witches?" I asked, trying to get back my earlier excitement. "*Real* witches?"

Mom looked at me in a way I didn't much like.

"Never mind," I said. "Stupid question."

The timer beeped, a noise that was very unwitchy. I waited until Mom's back was turned, then ducked out of the kitchen.

By six-thirty, Mom and Dad were putting the finishing touches on their Sonny and Cher outfits. Downstairs, Sandra was taping a Honey Nut Cheerios box to Ty's chest and a box of Product 19 to his back. Empty, of course. She planned to carry a kitchen knife in her hand and follow Ty from room to room. "I'll be a cereal killer," she told us during our dinner of crackers and cheese. "Get it?"

I was the only one who wasn't ready. I was going as a witch, of course, since that's what I went as every year. But I couldn't find the pointy hat to go with my long, black cape, and what good was a witch without a hat?

I plowed once more through the clothes in my closet, then backed out and plopped down on my bed. Sweetie-Pie leapt up beside me, and I scratched her jaw. "Where is it, Sweetie-Pie?" I asked. "Huh?"

Sweetie-Pie stepped on my thigh and rubbed harder against my hand.

"You can be my familiar," I told her. "*If* I can find that stupid hat."

I stood up, depositing Sweetie-Pie on the floor. Maybe Mom put the hat in the attic when she cleaned out my closet at the end of the summer. She'd bugged me for days to clean it out myself, but I never got around to it.

Sweetie-Pie followed me to the attic door. She yowled when I pressed her back with my foot.

"No, Sweetie-Pie," I said. "Stay." I wedged my body through the door, but Sweetie-Pie squirmed past me and bolted up the cluttered stairs.

"Sweetie-Pie! Get back here!"

"Winnie?" Mom called. "Is something wrong?"

I glanced up the attic stairs, then back at the bright light of the hall. "Uh, everything's fine! I'm just finishing getting ready!"

"Don't take too long," Mom said. "It's nearly seven!"

I stepped over a bag of old board games and gingerly made my way up the stairs. A dead cockroach crunched under my shoe, and I sucked in my breath. Dead cockroaches meant live cockroaches, and I *hated* live cockroaches.

"Sweetie-Pie!" I said. "Come here, Sweetie-Pie!"

Sweetie-Pie mewed, and I moved farther into the attic.

Lopsided stacks of boxes made spooky shapes against the walls, and the furnace hissed and popped. A chain dangled from a bare lightbulb, and I gave it a tug. Nothing.

"Sweetie-Pie?" I said tentatively. I knew no one was up there with me, but I didn't want to be any louder than I had to be. I stepped deeper into the darkness. "Come on, Sweetie-Pie. This isn't funny."

My arm brushed against something furry—*not* Sweetie-Pie—and I gasped. It was only a spiderweb, but it was gross and sticky and it made me think of giant tarantulas. My heart whammed against my chest. "All right, Sweetie-Pie, I'm leaving. If you get stuck up here, it's not my—"

From the back of the attic came a scuffling sound, followed by a bump and a howl.

"Sweetie-Pie?"

More howls, each one louder and more frantic than the one before. I decided this was not something I could handle on my own, and I clumped down the attic stairs as fast as I could. "Mom! Dad!" I cried. I raced to their bedroom. "It's Sweetie-Pie! I don't know what happened, but—"

"Winnie, slow down," Dad said. "Something happened to Sweetie-Pie?"

Sweetie-Pie howled again, only this time the sound came from behind Mom and Dad's wall. All three of us jumped, and Mom said, "What in the . . . is that *Sweetie-Pie?*"

"She snuck into the attic!" I said. "And there was this big noise and I don't know what happened and—"

"Dad!" Sandra yelled from downstairs. "Get down here! There's an animal trapped in the chimney!"

"The *chimney!*" Mom said.

We hurried to the den, where Sandra stood waving the poker at the fireplace. Ty clutched her leg and stared wide-eyed at the opening above the logs.

"I think it's a raccoon!" Sandra said. "Can you hear it?"

I didn't need to listen to know the answer. I stepped over the grate and stuck my head up the chimney. "Don't worry, Sweetie-Pie! We'll save you!"

"Sweetie-Pie?" Sandra said. "What's Sweetie-Pie doing in the fireplace?"

"Sweetie-Pie!" Ty cried. He let go of Sandra and climbed over the grate. "I'm sorry, Sweetie-Pie! I didn't know it was you!"

"She's not in the chimney," Dad said. He strode to the wall and rapped it with his knuckles. Sweetie-Pie moaned. "Hear that?" he said. "She must have slipped down between the panels of Sheetrock."

"Joel, do something," Mom said. "We can't have Sweetie-Pie making those noises during the party."

"The *party?*" I said. "Who cares about the party?"

Sweetie-Pie let out a whine that dipped up and down the scale. Mom pressed her hand to her mouth, but a giggle escaped through her fingers. "Oh, this is terrible. Everyone'll think we're animal torturers. Or worse."

I stomped my foot. "Mom!"

"Just tell them you stuck her down there on purpose," Sandra said. "It *is* a Halloween party."

"*San*-dra!"

"What? You're the one who let her into the attic."

Mom turned to Dad. "Can you get her out?"

"I don't know. I hope so." He put his hand on my shoulder. "Come on, Winnie. Let's see if we can rescue that cat of yours."

Armed with a flashlight apiece, we climbed the dusty attic stairs and picked our way toward the sound of Sweetie-Pie's cries.

"Be careful," Dad said. "We don't want you falling down a hole, too. Your mother would have a fit."

"Yeah, but only because I'd ruin the party."

Dad laughed. "A child in the wall—what would the neighbors think?"

I wasn't ready to joke. "I'm *not* a child."

We reached the far end of the attic. Crouching, we peered into the space between the walls.

"Sweetie-Pie?" Dad said. Her howls, which had tapered off, started back full force. He moved his flashlight. "There she is. See her?"

"Oh, poor Sweetie-Pie!" I said. She was at the bottom of a hole that stretched about a foot and a half across and maybe five feet down. Her eyes glowed in the beam of light, and she was covered with fluff and dust. She wailed and clawed at the siding.

"Here, hold this," Dad said, passing me his flashlight. With one arm braced on the floorboards, he leaned into the hole. "Okay, Sweetie-Pie, if you could just . . . no, now, hold on—"

He grunted and pushed himself up. "Can't reach her. Not even close." He brushed his hands on his jeans. "It'll have to be you, Winnie."

"Dad. If you can't reach her, there's no way I can."

"I'll hold on to your legs and lower you down," he said.

"What?!"

"Just don't tell your mother. She wouldn't like it."

She wouldn't like it? What about *me*?

On the other hand, if Dad thought I was brave enough to be lowered into the hole, then maybe I was. And I liked the part about not telling Mom—especially since I *could* tell Amanda and Chantelle and dumb old Gail Grayson. "Yeah," I'd say, "my dad and I decided to keep it a secret. We didn't want Mom to have a heart attack or anything."

I bet Gail has never been lowered headfirst into a gaping, pitch-black hole. A million dollars, that's how much I'd bet.

"Think you can do it?" Dad asked.

I gazed down at Sweetie-Pie, who scrabbled again at the siding. "Hold on," I told her. "I'm coming."

The first time we tried, I only managed to wiggle my head and outstretched arms into the hole. The Sheetrock dug into the skin beneath my armpits, and the air tasted like spiderwebs, which made me wonder what else had fallen into the hole over the years. I pushed the thought from my mind.

"Can you reach her?" Dad said.

"No. She's still, like, a couple of feet away."

"Okay. I'm going to lower you a little more." He shuffled forward, and I dipped deeper into the hole. My breath came fast in my chest.

"Now?" Dad asked.

I grazed Sweetie-Pie's paw as she batted at my fingers, but I still couldn't get hold of her.

"No good," I gasped. Something feathery brushed my lips, and I jerked away. "Pull me up!"

"What?"

"I said pull me up!"

His hands tightened on my calves. "Let's just try one more—"

"Pull me up now!"

He grunted and lifted me out of the hole, easing me onto the attic floor. I shuddered and brushed my hands over my legs, stomach, arms, and hair.

"I think I swallowed a spider," I said, pulling fuzz off my tongue with my fingers.

Dad shone his flashlight back down at Sweetie-Pie, who howled as if she thought we were going to leave her. "Well, what now?" he said.

I thought for several minutes. "Maybe we could lower a basket? You know, with some rope?"

Dad looked dubious, but he didn't say no. "You want to hunt one down?"

I got to my feet. "Be right back."

My bedroom was bright and cheerful compared to the attic. I dragged a chair into the closet and pulled an old Easter basket from the top shelf. A pointy black triangle fell down from behind it.

My witch's hat.

I stared at it, then shoved it in the corner behind my shoes.

"Winnie?" Mom called from downstairs. "We can still hear Sweetie-Pie crying! What's going on?"

I stepped into the hall and leaned over the banister. "I need some rope!"

"What for?"

Sandra joined Mom at the bottom of the stairs. "Why are you all dusty?" she asked. "Did you fall in, too?"

Ty came running from the den to see.

"I just need some rope," I said.

"Why?" Ty said.

I didn't want to explain in front of Sandra, because I knew she'd burst out laughing. But they were all standing there looking at me. "Because we're going to tie it to my Easter basket. We're going to make, like, an elevator so Sweetie-Pie can—"

Sandra burst out laughing. "An elevator?!"

The doorbell rang, and Mom's eyes flew to the door. "Check the drawer beneath the microwave. I think there's a ball of twine. And tell your father to hurry!"

I jogged downstairs to the kitchen. The twine was where Mom said it would be, but it didn't look strong enough to hold both Sweetie-Pie and the basket. I dropped it back in the drawer.

"Would this work?" Ty asked. He held out a yellow-and-white jump rope.

"Ty, that's perfect!" I said. I pulled it between my hands, testing its strength. "I'll bring it right back!"

I raced back to the attic, where I knotted one end of the rope around the handle of the Easter basket. "Can I be the one to lower it down?"

"It was your idea," Dad said. He aimed the flashlight toward Sweetie-Pie, and I eased the basket into the hole and let the rope slide through my fingers.

"Hold on, Sweetie-Pie," I called. "Almost there."

The rope stopped moving. Dad and I leaned forward.

"Uh-oh," I said.

Dad groaned. The basket sat smack-dab on top of Sweetie-Pie's head. She yowled, and Dad and I shared a look.

"Your mother is not going to be happy," he said.

I jiggled the rope. "Move, Sweetie-Pie."

She yowled again.

I reeled in the basket. "I have another idea," I said. "I'll be right back."

I dashed downstairs and got a can of tuna fish from the pantry, which I opened and scraped onto a paper plate. From the hall, I could hear people chatting. Something about baby raccoons being trapped in someone's chimney, which everyone seemed to find extremely hilarious.

"No luck?" Sandra said, breezing into the kitchen to grab a tray of hors d'oeuvres. "Mr. Miles is taking bets on how long it takes you guys to get her out. I told him about the elevator, and he doubled the stakes."

I brushed past her. Back in the attic, I told Dad to scoot over and let me have another try. Then I placed the tuna fish on the bottom of the basket, wedging the edge of the plate against the basket's side so it would stay in place. "Now she'll want to climb in," I explained.

I started to lower the basket, then paused and dropped down a small chunk of tuna by itself. Sweetie-Pie stopped mewing long enough to gobble it up, and I nodded. "You like that, huh? Well, here comes some more."

I lowered the basket. Again, it landed on Sweetie-Pie's head.

"Hmm," Dad said.

I jounced the basket to loosen the tuna-fish smell. "Go on," I said. "Get in."

"Maybe we should call the fire department. They get cats

out of trees. Maybe they can get cats out of attics." He drummed his fingers on the floor. "Have the guests started arriving?"

I jostled the rope. From beneath the basket, a paw swiped the air. "Come on, Sweetie-Pie," I whispered. Her head pushed between the basket and the Sheetrock, and in one quick burst she hopped over the wicker edge and onto the paper plate.

"She's in!" I said. I started to pull her up.

"Easy, now," Dad said. "Take your time."

Sweetie-Pie shifted her weight, and the basket lurched to the side. I held my breath.

"Steady," Dad said. "Just a little farther."

When the basket reached the top of the hole, Dad grabbed Sweetie-Pie and pinned her against his chest. "Got her."

"Sweetie-Pie!" I said. I scratched behind her ears, picking bits of fluff from her fur. Sweetie-Pie purred and butted my hand.

"Excellent job," Dad said. He heaved himself to his feet and motioned for me to grab the flashlights. "Come on. We've got a party to get to."

In the den, I passed around pizza eyeballs and tried to look modest as Dad told the story of Sweetie-Pie's rescue. Everyone seemed impressed when he got to the part about the tuna fish, and they laughed when he described how Sweetie-Pie tried to dash back up to the attic the minute he deposited her in the hall.

"Caught her by the tip of her tail," Dad said, shaking his head. "Crazy cat."

I looked at him from across the room. He winked at me, and I glowed with pride.

"My daughter has four cats," someone said beside me.

I turned to see Mr. Devine sipping a cup of punch.

"One of them got trapped in the pantry once. Took Dinah hours to hunt her down, because for some reason that cat doesn't meow. Never has."

"Huh," I said. It wasn't very exciting, a cat in the pantry. And what kind of cat didn't know how to meow?

"You should have seen her when Dinah finally found her," he said. "Purring and licking Dinah's face like Dinah was the greatest thing since chopped liver."

I smiled politely. Mr. Devine is short and pale, like Dinah, and he'd come to the party in blue-and-red Superman tights, which was kind of embarrassing because I could see the line of his underwear underneath. But he seemed nice.

I thought about Sweetie-Pie, how scared she was in that hole. I thought about Dinah's cat, so happy to be among people again.

"Um, Mr. Devine?" I said. I hesitated, then plunged ahead. "Do you think you could go get her? Dinah, I mean. I meant to invite her earlier, but I forgot."

"Sure," he said, nodding in a happy way. "She was thinking about watching the Peanuts special, but I know she'd rather come here."

That last part I pretended not to hear. I would die if Dad told anyone I watched the Great Pumpkin on TV. But maybe Dinah and I could watch it, if she really wanted to. I had enough Halloween to share.

November

AT HOME, MOM IS THE ONE who cooks our Thanksgiving meal, although Dad helps out by keeping us kids out of her hair while she bustles around. But for the big Thanksgiving feast at school, we kids did everything ourselves. The younger grades were in charge of decorations, the fourth graders made applesauce, the fifth graders churned butter, and the sixth graders baked bread. On the day of the feast itself, everyone wore clothes that were fancier than normal, and it was fun to see everyone all polished and spiffed up. I wore a black corduroy skirt and a soft white cardigan, and I put on my ring with the greenish-blue stone that I saved for special occasions.

"Ooo," Amanda said when she saw it. "It's the color of the ocean after a storm."

"Yeah," I said. I stared at her hair. Yesterday it reached below her waist, but today it fell in smooth layers around her face, just like Gail's. She'd even gone to Gail's stylist to get it done—a place I'd never heard of called the Van Michael Salon. "I can't believe you cut it," I said. "You've been growing it for so long."

"The stylist said a shorter style would be better for my face. Don't you like it?"

I didn't have to answer, because right then Gail bounded up and threw her arm over Amanda's shoulder.

"Amanda, come on! Ms. Russell's doing the seating chart for the feast, and I'll die if she doesn't put us together."

"You guys have to have a seating chart?" I said. "Mr. Hutchinson said we were mature enough to choose our own seats."

Gail looked me over. "Winnie," she said. "Hi."

"Show Gail your ring," Amanda said.

I held out my hand, and Gail stepped closer. "Is it an emerald?" she asked. She peered at the stone. "Oh."

"What?"

"Nothing. It's just . . . it's not an emerald, that's all."

"So?"

"So, nothing." She flipped her hair away from her face. "My birthstone's an emerald. I feel really lucky, because what if it was, like, an opal? Or a *garnet?*"

"Mine's a sapphire," Amanda said.

"Mine's an aquamarine," I said. I wiggled my ring. "That's what this is."

"An aquamarine's not a gem, though," Gail said. "Not actually."

That was one of the most ridiculous things I'd ever heard. Aquamarines are beautiful. They're what mermaids would

wear if mermaids wore jewelry. Anyway, what about the
Aqua Girls, whom Gail had been so fired up about just two
months ago? A real Aqua Girl would definitely wear an
aquamarine.

I opened my mouth to point this out, then changed my
mind. Gail could say whatever she wanted. I wasn't going to
let her take my ring's specialness away.

Gail tugged on Amanda's arm. "Come *on*," she said. "The
bell's going to ring any second!"

I watched them sprint down the hall and tried not to feel
left out. Who cared if Gail and Amanda had better birth-
stones than me? And who cared if they'd be eating bread
and applesauce side by side, giggling and fluffing their twin
haircuts?

But it hurt to think of them doing things together. Whispering at the salon, waltzing out arm in arm with their
fresh-smelling hair. Other stuff, too—I knew because twice
I'd called Amanda over the weekend, and both times her
mom said she was at a friend's. "Who?" I asked the first
time. The second time, I just said "oh" and hung up. It made
my stomach feel hollow, realizing there were parts of Amanda's life I no longer knew about.

Then again, there were parts of my life Amanda didn't
know about, either. Like the fact that this afternoon I was
going home with Dinah Devine, and that her dad was going
to drop us off at the mall so we could visit the kittens in the

pet store. We both thought it was terrible how those kittens had to be penned in a cage for their entire lives, or at least until someone bought them. We knew we couldn't take them home with us—Mom said absolutely no more pets, and Dinah's dad said four cats were enough, thank you very much—but we could still talk to them and make scratchy noises with our fingers. We figured that had to count for something.

If Amanda hadn't dashed off with Gail, would I have told her about Dinah? Not that it mattered, since she did dash off.

The warning bell rang. I hitched my backpack over my shoulder and hurried down the empty hall.

"Here you go, girls," Dinah's dad said, handing us each a ten-dollar bill. "Have fun. I'll pick you up at five-thirty in front of the Chick-fil-A."

"Don't forget about your dry cleaning," Dinah said. "And you're supposed to call Charlie about the roof, remember? Tell him Saturday's better than Sunday, but not until after ten." She waved until the car was out of sight, then turned to me. "So. Kittens first, or shopping?"

I didn't answer. I stared at the money in my hand, and then at her. "Here," I said, thrusting the bill in front of me.

"What? No, it's yours."

"What for?"

She shrugged. "To spend."

"But—" I shut my mouth. If Mr. Devine wanted to give me ten dollars, fine. But it made me uneasy, like the time I visited Great-Grandmother Robinson in the nursing home, and she gave me a wrinkled five-dollar bill from her plastic change purse. Like she thought she had to pay me for coming to see her.

"Kittens," I said at last, stuffing the money in my pocket. "Let's go."

The cutest kitten in the bunch, we both agreed, was a tiny white puffball with gray eyes. Her paws were the color of soot, so we named her Cinders, short for Cinderella.

"Which is perfect," Dinah said. "After all, she's kind of an orphan, too, just like the real Cinderella."

"Poor thing," I said. "Can you imagine how horrible it would be to be this teeny, little thing and not even have your mother to take care of you?"

Dinah got all quiet, and I realized what I'd said.

"Not you," I blurted. "I mean, yes, you, but—"

"I know. It's okay."

I felt bad even though she said that. I wrapped my arms around my ribs and said, "Do you . . . remember her? Your mom?"

She pressed her knuckle against the side of the glass cage. "A little."

I waited for her to continue, but she didn't say anything

more. I turned back to Cinders. "Look. She's trying to bat your finger."

"I wish I could hold her," Dinah said. She squatted so that she was closer to the floor of the cage. "Do you know how to say 'I love you' to a cat? You blink three times really slowly, like this."

She blinked three times, and Cinders meowed.

Dinah smiled. "See? You have to think the words *I love you* as you do it. Otherwise, it won't work."

"You girls want that white one?" the owner of the store asked. He regarded us from over the tops of his glasses.

Dinah stood up. "We're just looking."

"Well, other people want to look, too. You've been camped in front of that cage for half an hour."

Dinah spread her hand out flat against the side of the cage. "Don't worry," she said to Cinders. "Someone nice is going to buy you. Someone who'll take good care of you, I promise."

"She's deaf," the store owner said. "Can't hear a word you say."

I glanced at Dinah, who was holding her mouth in a stiff kind of way. "How can you tell?" I asked. "I mean, are you sure?"

"Sure I'm sure. White cats are almost always deaf—some sort of screwy wiring in their genes." He took off his glasses and rubbed the bridge of his nose. "Too bad, but that's the way it goes."

Dinah stood before the cage for another minute, then let her hand fall from the glass.

At The Gap, Dinah inspected a pile of sweaters while I rifled through the sales rack.

"Look," I said, holding up a lime-green button-down. "Isn't this cute?"

She stepped out from behind the sweater display, and I remembered what of course I'd known before: that Dinah is not the person to consult when it came to matters of fashion. Today she wore a sagging yellow dress with a nubbly blue cardigan buttoned over the front. On the pocket of the cardigan was a pony.

She squinted at the shirt. "It's nice. Do you want to try it on?"

"Nah. It's a large—it would be too big." I almost suggested *she* try it on, but I caught myself at the last second. I couldn't help thinking, though, what a difference it would make if she wore normal clothes. Not to me, but to the other kids at school.

"Hey, want to go look at the jeans?" I said. "We could both try some on. It would be fun."

Her eyebrows shot up. She glanced around the store, then giggled and jammed her hands under her armpits. "Okay, sure."

I grabbed a pair of carpenter jeans for me—I knew they'd

swallow me, but who cared—and helped Dinah pick out two pairs of relaxed fits, one with frayed cuffs and one just plain normal. We chose adjoining stalls in the dressing room, and as I stepped out of my corduroys, I could hear Dinah giggling in that same nervous way as when I first brought up the idea.

"What's so funny?" I asked.

I heard the sound of a zipper being zipped, followed by a grunt. And then more giggles.

"Dinah?"

"I don't think this is the way they're supposed to look. Will you come check?"

I pulled on my jeans, clutched the fabric at the waist so they'd stay on, and slipped into the hall. "Let's see."

She cracked her door and yanked me in. "They're too big, I'm pretty sure. Or maybe too small? And why are they so long? Is that normal?" She glanced at my face, and her cheeks turned red. She started undoing the buttons. "That bad, huh? I should have known. I guess I'm just not a—"

"Wait!" I said. "Just . . . wait! The jeans are fine. It's just . . ."

I exhaled. It was just that she'd taken off her dress in order to try them on, which meant she was naked from the waist up. Naked and smooth and white, except for two pink nipples like dots of jam.

I focused on her hips, on the bulge of flesh above the waist of her jeans. "I'll get a shirt for you to try them with. Be right back."

I grabbed the first shirt I saw, a soft blue V-neck printed with tiny daisies. But I stopped outside Dinah's stall and pressed my back against the wall. Occasionally I saw Mom naked, like if I needed to ask her a question when she was taking a bath, but even then she was mostly underwater. And Sandra always shut her door before undressing. Amanda and I turned our backs if we changed in the same room, and if one of us happened to see anything, we quickly looked away.

It wasn't that being naked was *bad*. It was just embarrassing. Other kids knew that without being told. Why didn't Dinah?

Gail Grayson, if she saw Dinah without a shirt on . . .

I didn't want to think about it. Once Maxine came back from the bathroom with the bottom of her skirt tucked partway into her tights, and Gail gasped and said, "Maxine! You're *showing!*" If she whispered it, that would have been one thing, but she said it so loud that everyone in the cafeteria turned to stare.

I knocked on Dinah's stall and passed the shirt over the top of the door. Five seconds later, Dinah came out and stood before the three full-sized mirrors at the end of the dressing room. She stared at herself straight on, then turned sideways and examined her profile. Her hands flitted from her stomach to her hips, gentle as little birds.

"You look good," I said.

"Really?" Her expression reminded me of Ty, the way he furrowed his brow when he hoped I'd watch *Rugrats* with him.

"Really. You look awesome."

She studied her reflection once more. The loose fit of the jeans made her seem thinner than she actually is, and the daisies on the shirt brought out the rosiness of her skin. "My dad's supposed to take me shopping over the weekend. Maybe I'll bring him here."

"Yeah, you should." I tilted my head. "Have you never tried on clothes here before?"

Dinah blushed. "I started to once or twice. But . . . I don't know. Everything's always in such neat stacks. I didn't want to mess them up."

"Dinah. It's a store. You're *supposed* to mess them up."

She straightened her shoulders. "Well, now I know."

I spent the money Mr. Devine gave me at the Candy Bin. Usually I only bought a dollar's worth of Jelly-Bellies or a couple of giant jawbreakers, but today I let myself go wild. Malted milk balls, white chocolate truffles, spice drops shaped like seashells—anything I wanted, I put in my bag.

Twenty feet away, Dinah pored over the jewelry at one of the wooden carts by the fountain. Every once in a while I glanced out of the store to make sure she was still there, and each time I saw her peering at the velvet display trays with a determined frown.

At 5:15, she appeared by my side clutching a small brown bag. "We should go," she said. "Sometimes my dad is early."

I paid for my candy, and we wound our way through the food court until we reached the Chick-fil-A. Out front, a white-haired lady offered bites of chicken on toothpicks, and we took one apiece. We checked for samples at the Great American Cookie Company, but the plate on the counter was empty.

"You know where we should have gone?" Dinah said as she settled into a white plastic chair. "The Cinnabon in the basement of Macy's. They always give out samples, and each sample is, like, practically an entire cinnamon roll."

"Mmm."

"Maybe next time," she said.

"Sure, that sounds good."

She folded the top of her bag over, then folded it once more. She creased the edge with her fingernail. "You know how you asked about my mom? If I remembered her?"

Her question took me by surprise, because I hadn't thought about that since we left the pet store. But I nodded.

"Well, I don't. Not really. I was only four months old when she died."

I swallowed. "That's awful."

"Yeah. But anyway, it's weird. I *try* to remember her, but

I end up thinking about my dad, instead. Like how he raised me all by himself, even though he knew nothing about babies."

I imagined Mr. Devine in his Halloween tights. I imagined him holding a little baby. "Dinah—"

"It's okay, though. I mean, he figured it out and stuff." She lifted her head and thrust the paper bag across the table. "Here. This is for you."

I opened the bag. Inside was a bracelet woven from blue and gold thread.

"It's a friendship bracelet," Dinah said.

"I know." I pulled it out and turned it over in my hands. You were supposed to make this kind of bracelet, not buy it, but I didn't tell Dinah that. "Thanks," I said. "And, uh, this is for you." I handed her my bag of candy with only a small ping of regret.

She peered inside. "Wow! Thanks! I *love* malted milk balls." She popped one into her mouth. "Want me to tie your bracelet on for you? You're supposed to wear it until it falls off on its own. It's good luck."

If I wore it, Amanda would notice. So would Gail. And I knew she'd make some comment about it, like she did about my ring. If I could tell the bracelet was store-bought, then it was a snap that Gail would, too.

Even if she didn't, she was sure to ask who gave it to me.

But I liked Dinah. So what if she doesn't always know the

right way to do things? She's nice. She's brave, in ways that not everyone knows about. And she knows how to say "I love you" to cats.

I pushed the bracelet across the table and held out my arm.

December

THE DAY OF THE SNOWSTORM, Alex Plotkin ate a dried-up bumblebee that he found on Mr. Hutchinson's windowsill. It was like the time he ate the raw egg, only worse, because the bee crunched.

"Ew!" Maxine said, scooting away her desk. "Don't you breathe on me, Alex. Don't you dare!"

"Way to go," Ross Gallivan said. He slapped Alex's hand and cracked up. "You've got, like, a foot hanging out of your mouth."

"That's sick," Maxine said. "Bees don't have feet."

"Well, something's hanging out," Ross said.

Dinah pressed her knuckles to her mouth, and I giggled. We'd been spending more and more time together, and one of the things I liked about her was how easily she got grossed out.

"Winnie, he ate a bee," she said, like she still couldn't believe it.

"At least it was dead," I said.

"Still . . ." She peeked again at Alex. "Think about his

poor wife one day. Alex's, not the bee's. She'll have to kiss that very same mouth!"

"Unlikely," I said. "You really think anyone's going marry him?"

That made her laugh.

Mr. Hutchinson strode into the room and took in all the commotion. "What's going on in here? Someone want to fill me in?"

I looked at Dinah. Last year, she would have told, but this year, she sealed her lips with the rest of us.

Mr. Hutchinson raked his hand through his hair. "All right. Not important. Listen up: The weather stations are predicting five inches of snow by this afternoon, and Mrs. Jacobs has decided to dismiss school early. She had Jeanie call the radio stations and Channel Two, and they'll spread the word. Your parents should be here to pick you up at noon."

It took a second for his words to sink in, and then a cheer erupted from the entire class. Up and down the hall, stomps and whistles filled the air as other classes received the news.

Dinah raised her hand.

"Yes, Dinah?"

"What if my dad's not listening to the radio when they make the announcement?"

"Jeanie's calling parents in each of the grades, and they'll activate the PTA phone trees. But don't worry, several of the teachers will stay until everyone's been picked up."

"Could I go call him, just to make sure?"

Mr. Hutchinson almost said no, I could tell, but then he looked outside at the heavy, gray clouds. "Okay," he said, "but make it quick. Anyone else need to make a call? Raise your hands and I'll let you go one by one."

I wasn't worried about Mom getting the message—she always knew about bake sales and field trips and stuff like that—so I stayed in the room and played Seven-Up with the rest of the class.

At a little after 10:00, Karen shrieked and pointed at the window. Everyone dashed to see, even the people with their heads on their desks who were supposed to have their eyes shut. Furry white flakes fell from the sky. They dusted the jungle gym and the black rubber swings, and within seconds they blurred the line between the basketball court and the rest of the playground.

"Awesome!" Alex said.

"It's really coming down," said Ross. "Look how thick it is on the sidewalk!"

Karen and Louise grabbed hands and jumped up and down, squealing about the snowman they'd make when they got home. Maxine said she was going to make snow candy with maple syrup, like Mary and Laura in *Little House on the Prairie*.

The snow continued to fall.

"I've never seen anything like this," Mr. Hutchinson said.

"Not in Atlanta. People are going to have a heck of a time on the roads if the temperature keeps dropping."

"It looks like a blizzard," Dinah said in a low voice. She pressed her forehead against the window. "Maybe we'll all be trapped."

"We won't be trapped," I said. But I shivered, enjoying the possibility. I was glad Ty stayed home from kindergarten today. I knew he'd be safe and snug with Mom.

At 11:45 we traipsed to the gym in a noisy clump, peering out the hall windows to check the status of the storm. By now the ground was entirely white, and the cars in the faculty parking lot were soft, humpbacked monsters without a hint of glass or metal showing through.

"Sixth graders on the far wall," Mrs. Jacobs instructed. "Sit down and stay down. Your teacher will call you when your parents are here."

Ms. Russell's class had already arrived, and I sprinted across the floor to find Amanda and Chantelle. Gail was there, too, but there wasn't anything I could do about it.

"Can you believe it?" I said. I dropped down beside them. "Mr. Hutchinson says it's five inches deep already. He says if it ices over, we're really in trouble."

"Five inches is nothing," Gail said. "In Chicago, we got, like, fourteen inches all the time. I don't know what everyone's making such a big deal about."

"Yeah, but this is Atlanta," I said. "Last year it didn't

snow at all, and the year before there was a teeny bit but not even enough to make a snowman."

"Not even enough to make a snowbaby," Chantelle said. "We tried."

"Mrs. Jacobs said traffic's backed up all the way to Moore's Mill," Dinah said. She stood before us, twisting her hands. "She said the roads are totally blocked."

"So?" Gail said. "The snowplows will be able to get through."

"We don't have snowplows in Atlanta," Amanda said.

Dinah sucked on a strand of her pale hair. She looped it around her fingers and pulled it out. "Can I sit here? With you?"

Gail shot Chantelle a look, and embarrassment rose inside me. Then I got mad at myself for feeling that way and said, "Of course. You don't have to ask, you know." It wasn't Dinah's fault Gail was a jerk. Still, I wished it were as easy being friends with Dinah in a crowd as it was when we were alone.

I turned to Amanda. "Maybe your mom will let you spend the night. We could make hot chocolate."

"And snow angels," Amanda said.

"In Chicago, we made snow angels all the time," Gail said. "Me and Annie, this girl from school? We made thirteen snow angels one winter, all holding hands. Her mom said it was the most beautiful thing she'd ever seen."

Dinah checked her watch. "It's ten after twelve. Why isn't my dad here?"

"She called him from the office," I told the others, feeling like I had to explain her anxiousness. "He promised he'd leave right away."

"Ms. Russell wouldn't let anyone call home," Chantelle said. "She said if one kid wanted to use the phone, then everyone would, and Mrs. Jacobs would have a fit."

"Don't you think calling home is kind of babyish?" Gail said. "That's what Ms. Russell said."

I bit my lip. Ms. Russell would never have used the word *babyish,* and we all knew it.

"Well, Mr. Hutchinson let me," Dinah said. "And my dad said he'd be here."

"He'll come," I said. "Don't worry."

She gave me a smile, which I didn't deserve.

At 1:30, the gym was still full. Every so often a red-cheeked mom or dad would come in from the cold to claim a waiting kid, but in the last half hour only three moms and one grandfather had pushed through the heavy gym doors.

"There's ice everywhere," Maxine's mom told Mr. Hutchinson. "I saw seven cars skid off the road at the intersection of Habersham and West Wesley. Bam-bam-bam, until they were scrunched together like pop-beads. And a red Mercedes plowed into the signal pole, so now the light's out." She tightened her scarf around her neck. "Come on, Maxine. It'll only get worse the longer we wait."

At 2:00, the teachers passed out milk and graham crackers from the cafeteria, and at 2:45 we filed grade by grade to the bathroom. At 3:15, with the snow still falling, Mr. Hutchinson and Ms. Russell leaned together and murmured uneasily.

"—fold their jackets and use them as pillows," I heard Mr. Hutchinson say. "And I switched the thermostat off automatic, so the building will stay warm. We just better hope the furnace keeps running."

Ms. Russell nodded and said something about ice-cream sandwiches left over from last year's Field Day. "And activities," she added. "We'll have to think up some games to keep these kids entertained." She caught me listening and smiled reassuringly. "Nothing to worry about, Winnie. Just planning for contingencies."

She and Mr. Hutchinson stepped farther away, and I turned back to Amanda and the others.

"Did you hear?" I said. "We might have to spend the night!"

"What?" Dinah said. Her chest rose and fell. "I can't spend the night here. I don't have my retainer!"

"It won't matter for one night," Amanda said.

"And what about brushing my teeth? I don't even have my toothbrush!"

"Nobody does," Gail said. "We'll have to use our fingers."

"Our *fingers?*"

"You're not going to die," Gail said. "Grow up."

I dug my fingernails into my palms, hating Gail's scornful tone. It made me mad, but it was a tight-stomach kind of mad, because it wasn't as if I was jumping to Dinah's defense. Even though I wanted to, something held me back.

The door opened at the other side of the gym. A man came in and brushed the snow from his coat.

"Anyway, you won't have to worry about it," I said to Dinah. "Look."

"Dad!" she cried. She ran to meet him. "What took you so long?"

Gail watched as Mr. Devine gave Dinah a hug. Then she took her brush from her purse and ran it through her hair. "Thank God. Spending an entire night with Dinah—now *that* would be a nightmare."

"That's mean," I made myself say. "Dinah's not so bad."

Gail's brush stopped midstroke. "Well, you would know, wouldn't you?"

I didn't answer.

Dinah and her father headed our way, Dinah holding her dad's hand and grinning from ear to ear.

"My dad helped rescue a Ford Taurus that got stuck at the bottom of a hill," she said. "Only he slipped, which is why he's all wet. He says cars are stuck *everywhere*. One lady even left her groceries in the backseat so she could walk home, except for a package of fudge-stripe cookies, which she shared with anyone who was hungry. Wasn't that nice?"

"Thrilling," Gail said, low enough so Dinah's dad couldn't hear.

"Anyway," Dinah continued, "we can give you guys a ride home if you want. Or you can all spend the night at my house. My dad says it's okay." She looked at me. "You want to, Winnie? We have hot chocolate mix, the kind with marshmallows."

"Um, thanks, but I'm sure my mom's on the way. She'll probably be here any minute." My face felt hot, and I knew I was blushing.

Gail cleaned her fingernails.

Chantelle stared at the boys playing basketball.

"I better wait, too," Amanda said softly. "But thanks for asking."

"Oh," Dinah said. Two spots of color rose on her cheeks.

"Another time," Mr. Devine said. He squeezed Dinah's hand. "Come on, sweetheart. Let's go."

Four o'clock came and went with no sign of Mom.

Five o'clock—still no Mom. At 5:30, Chantelle's dad arrived, and Chantelle didn't even pretend to be sad to leave. What had started off feeling like an adventure had stopped being fun about the same time Alex Plotkin nailed Louise with the basketball and Mrs. Jacobs made everyone sit down on the floor and rest, no talking allowed. She let us talk again after fifteen minutes, but by then everyone's mood had changed. Maybe it was the light coming in though the windows, gray and thin. Or maybe, like me, the others were thinking about dinner and their own warm beds. Part of me thought it would be exciting to spend the night in the gym, but a bigger part of me wanted chicken pot pie and the smell of Dad's Old Spice. Or if I couldn't have that, then at least a soft blanket and a pillow not made from my winter coat.

I should have gone home with Dinah.

At 6:15, Mr. Hutchinson interrupted a two-against-one game of Hang Man (Amanda and Gail were the two; I was the one) to tell me that Mom had called. She'd slid off the road on the way back from the mall, and it had taken her all this time to walk home.

"She said to tell you she's fine, and so is Ty."

"Is she on her way?" I asked.

"Her car's stuck at the mall," Mr. Hutchinson explained. "Your sister's boyfriend—Bo?—is coming for you in his Jeep." He turned to Amanda. "You're to go with Winnie. Winnie's mom passed on the message."

"Yay!" I said. "Hurray for Bo!"

Amanda clasped her hands to her heart. "My hero!"

"He's not here *yet*," Gail said. She drew a square around the letters I'd guessed wrong and started shading it in. "Are we going to finish the game or not?"

Amanda and I glanced at each other. When Bo picked us up, Gail would be left alone.

"Winnie," Amanda said, "maybe you could call your mom and—"

"*B*," I said to Gail.

"Nope," Gail said. She drew a foot on the stick figure hanging from the gallows, adding a shoe with a crisscross of laces. "You're dead."

"So what was the word?"

"Blind."

"But you said there were no *B*s!"

"I said there were no *P*s."

"I didn't say *P*. I said *B*!"

She folded the piece of paper and shoved it in her backpack. "Don't be a sore loser. It's just a game."

Outraged, I turned to Amanda.

"I wasn't really listening," she said in a small voice. She didn't mention calling my mom again.

It was after 7:00 by the time Bo straggled in. When I spotted him, I jumped to my feet. "He's here! Come on!"

Amanda slipped her backpack over her shoulder, then stood there fooling with the strap. "Your dad'll show up soon," she said to Gail.

"I know," Gail said. She'd glanced at Bo when he first came in, and she'd gotten a funny look on her face. But now she was smooth as could be. "He probably got stuck behind some dumbbell who doesn't know how to brake on ice."

I narrowed my eyes, because I knew who she was referring to. Still, Amanda and I were going home, and she
wasn't. For maybe the first time in her life, Gail would be
the one left behind.

Bo strode across the gym and swung me up in a hug.
"Have you been outside yet, Winnie? Have you seen how
crazy it is?"

I breathed in the cold smell of him. "Are you kidding?
The teachers wouldn't let us."

"It's absolutely nuts. And all those Saabs and Hondas and
dinky little VWs? They're *nothing* compared to the Jeep.
The Jeep rules."

"Where's Sandra?"

"She's at your house, making fudge for when we get back."

I clapped my hands. "Amanda, did you hear that? Sandra's making fudge!"

"My mom makes the best fudge in the world," Gail said.

I'd almost forgotten she was there.

"Once she won a year's supply of Marshmallow Fluff,"
she continued. "That's how good her recipe is."

I wanted to say something in return, like "Yeah? Well,
Sandra won a lifetime supply of Marshmallow Fluff. Our
pantry is *stuffed* with Marshmallow Fluff."

Bo hit his palm with his fist. "Come on, let's do it," he
said. "I left the motor running."

Amanda's hands fell to her sides. "Well," she said to Gail.
"Bye."

"See you," Gail said, like it was all pretty boring.

At the door, I stopped and looked back. Over by the basketball net, Mr. Hutchinson was playing a game of Horse with the remaining sixth-grade boys. The circles under his eyes had grown more pronounced, but his smile seemed real. A few feet away, Louise and Karen practiced their Holiday Pageant roles with a couple of fifth-grade girls. And in the far corner, all by herself, sat Gail. Leaning back on her palms, she pointed and flexed her feet.

I bit my lip. Deep down, I knew Gail wasn't *all* bad. Sometimes I watched her paint Amanda's fingernails, and I'd seen how carefully she brushed on the polish, like she really wanted to do a good job. And once Amanda told me how the two of them danced around like rock stars when they hung out at Gail's condominium. At the time I rolled my eyes, but I guess I could see how it might be fun.

If I wanted, I could still call Mom. It would only take a second.

But I didn't.

Outside, everything was blue-white and sparkling. Bo's Jeep sat by the curb, and from the front seat, Amanda waved for me to hurry. I closed the door to the gym and crunched through the crystally snow.

January

I DON'T KNOW WHAT IT'S LIKE in other places, but in Atlanta, we have outdoor recess all year long—even in shivery-cold January. And actually, it isn't *always* shivery cold. If the sun was out and the sky was clear, kids would shrug out of their coats and push up the sleeves of their new sweaters, eager for the feel of skin against air. And even when frost whitened the basketball court, well, it hardly mattered. We raced to the playground just the same, and for thirty spectacular minutes we played with Louise's Chinese jump rope.

The girls, anyway. The boys wanted nothing to do with it. Tyrone tried it once on a dare, but he messed up on the first round and stalked away. "Sheez," he said, shaking his head. "Chinese *jump rope?* That's no jump rope, it's a giant rubber band. Chinese rubber band, they should call it!"

Except it wasn't a rubber band. It was more like a giant ponytail holder, the kind with thread covering the elastic so it doesn't pull at your hair. Louise had gotten it in her Christmas stocking. This is how it worked: Two girls faced each other, not too close, and stood with their feet shoulder length apart. They looped the Chinese jump rope around their ankles, making a big, elastic rectangle about four inches off the ground. Then the girl whose turn it was moved into place. She had to jump the same pattern every time: in, out, side to side, in, on, scoop. Her feet couldn't touch the rope at all, except for the "on" part, when she had to land on top of the rope so that each foot smushed one side to the ground. Then came "scoop," which was the hardest part of all. For "scoop," she lifted one foot, hooked the rope with her toe, and pulled it over to the part held down by her other foot. Then she had to leap free of the whole caboodle and land back at the beginning, all without falling on her face.

"Scoop" was the bane of my existence. *If* by some miracle I got all the way to "on" without messing up, and *if* at that point I didn't start giggling and lose my balance, I always, always managed to snarl myself in the rope when it came to the actual scooping. Not even Louise got "scoop" right every time. In fact, to everyone's surprise, the best scooper in the grade was Dinah Devine. With her wide, flat feet and sensible white Keds, she hooked the rope as if she were born to it, and when she leapt free, it was like watching a knot unravel with a single pull. No tangle, no mess—just one happy Dinah with flushed, excited cheeks.

"I could do it, too, if it weren't for these shoes," Gail said. She scowled at her black Doc Martens with the clunky heels, as if she weren't the one who put them on that morning to match her embroidered jeans and turtleneck. "Stupid boots."

Dinah sailed her way through another perfect round, and everyone shook their heads. "Wow!" they said, and "Did you *see* that?" and "How do you do it?"

I was a teeny bit jealous, but mainly I felt proud. I clapped and said, "Go, Dinah!"

"It's time to move to the next level," Louise said. She slid her feet together so that her ankles touched, and motioned for Maxine to do the same. Now the rectangle was long and skinny instead of long and fat. "Okay, Dinah. You have to do the exact same pattern, only your feet *still* can't touch the rope."

Dinah glanced around the circle, pleased and embarrassed. She stepped up next to the rope. *In, out, side to side, in, on, scoop.*

"You did it!" I cried. I turned to Amanda. "She did it!"

"She did it," Gail mimicked. "Big whup. If it weren't for these boots . . ."

"Now up high," Louise said. She and Maxine tugged the jump rope over their shins and anchored it at their knees. Louise replanted her feet about six inches apart, and Maxine followed suit. "First you do it while our feet are spread, and then with them close together, just like down low. Then comes doubles down low and doubles up high, where you have to do everything twice, and then comes spins, where every time you jump you have to spin from front to back.

And then comes double spins, which not even my cousin from California can do."

I tried to imagine jumping into the air, spinning around, and landing with one foot on either length of the rope, all with the rope twelve inches off the ground. And then jumping up and doing it again, only this time landing so that you faced the opposite direction. Just thinking about it made my head hurt.

"Are you ready?" Louise said.

"Yeah," Gail said. "We're waiting."

Dinah studied the rope, squinting her eyes as if memorizing its height from the ground. She wiped her hands on her jeans and stepped into place. *In, out, side to side, in, on—*

Everyone breathed out in a whoosh.

"Oh, no," Louise said.

"Too bad," said Gail.

Dinah stared at the left side of the rope, which had popped free from her sneaker before she made it to "scoop."

"So close," I said. "You'll get it next time."

"Yeah, but now it's Sheila's turn," Gail said. She nudged Sheila forward. "Go."

Dinah left the center of the circle and took her place by my side.

"You were amazing," I told her.

She tugged a piece of hair to her mouth, then glanced at me in a sideways kind of way. She grinned.

⌒ ⌒ ⌒

The next day Gail showed up in a new pair of red-and-white Nikes, which she wore with white jeans and a soft white sweater. A bright red headband held back her hair.

"Me first," she said as Louise handed one end of the rope to Karen. She tapped her foot.

"Okay," Louise said. "We're ready."

Gail strode to her place. *In, out, side to side, in, on, scoop.*

"Yay!" Amanda said, along with several others. "Way to go!"

Louise and Karen shifted to the second position, the rope down low but their feet touching.

In, out, side to side, in, on, scoop.

"Yes!" said Chantelle.

"Now comes the hard one," Louise said. She and Karen hiked the rope over their knees and widened their stance.

Gail lifted her chin. *In, out, side to side, in, on, scoop.*

A cheer erupted from the circle of girls. Dinah's eyes found mine.

"My cousin said it took her forever to get that one," Louise said.

"Today I'm wearing the right shoes," Gail said. "Anyone can do it in the right shoes."

Louise scooted her knees together. "Are you ready for level four?"

"Of course."

Gail made it all the way to doubles up high before catching her foot in one of the side-to-sides. Her mouth tightened, and for a second she looked really upset. Then she smoothed her features and freed herself from the rope.

"You're next," she said, arching her eyebrows at Dinah.

Dinah blinked.

Louise and Karen put the rope back in position, and Dinah moved to the center of the circle. Down low wide, down low skinny. Up high wide, up high skinny. Then doubles down low, which looked impossible to me, but which Dinah cruised through without missing a step. Then doubles up high, the round Gail stumbled on. If Dinah made it through doubles up high, she would once more be the champ.

Gail gnawed on her knuckle.

Chantelle shifted from foot to foot.

And Amanda watched Dinah with a troubled expression. Not like she wanted Dinah to mess up, but like she knew how Gail would react if Dinah didn't.

"Come on, Dinah," I said. "You can do it."

Amanda looked at me, and my face grew hot. Somehow, even though officially we were still friends, Amanda and I had never talked about all the stuff she did with Gail, or the stuff I did with Dinah. Or the stuff we no longer did with each other. But the way she gazed at me made me understand how different things were between us, even if we didn't admit it.

Would Amanda say Gail was her new best friend, if someone asked?

Would I say Dinah was mine?

Dinah concentrated on her jumps, her forehead lined with worry. She poked her tongue in the space between her teeth and her lower lip, and each time she got a jump right, she let out a huff of air. On "double on" she almost lost her balance, but she thrust out her arms and stayed in place. She breathed in deep. Then scoop once, scoop twice, and everyone went crazy, clapping and cheering and calling her name.

Well, not everyone. Not Gail, and not Chantelle. And Amanda's claps were out of politeness. I could see it in the stiffness of her spine.

And me? I clapped until my palms stung, but it no longer felt the same.

I stayed in my room all evening, and when Dinah called, I told her I was doing my homework and couldn't talk. I thought about calling Amanda, but I didn't. Because what I'd realized was that there was no way things could go back to the way they were. Too much had changed. But it hadn't sunk in until today at recess, when I looked at the circle of sixth-grade girls and no longer knew my place.

If only Dinah were more . . . I don't know. If only she were more like Amanda, without actually *being* Amanda. Like maybe she could be the one everyone wanted to sit next to, instead of the one who smushed her sandwich under the lid of the heavy metal milk cooler, spurting herself with mayonnaise. And maybe she could stop doing that thing with her tongue and lower lip, because I'm sure she didn't know it, but it looked pretty dumb. She shouldn't giggle so much, either. Or chew her hair.

I knew I was horrible for thinking these things, but I couldn't stop. Because sure, everyone liked Dinah now, because right now she was queen of Chinese jump rope. But everyone liked Amanda just because she was Amanda. And when I was Amanda's best friend, they liked me that same way, too.

But if Dinah was my best friend, and I was hers . . .

That was the part that scared me. It was like last year at my birthday party, when no one wanted Dinah in her group. I wanted to be Dinah's friend, but I wanted to be part of the group as well.

I wanted both.

"Winnie!" Dinah said Wednesday morning. She ran down the hall to greet me, even though I would have reached the room in less than ten seconds. "You didn't get here and you didn't get here, and I thought maybe you were sick, which would be awful. You're not sick, are you?"

I hugged my books and veered slightly to the left. I could smell her breath. Strawberry Pop-Tart.

"Are you? Oh, no. Do you have a fever?" She placed her hand on my forehead, and I twisted away.

"I'm fine," I said. "Sheez, Dinah. The warning bell hasn't even rung yet."

"But usually you're here by seven forty-five. I got worried."

I walked into Mr. Hutchinson's room, and she followed me to my desk.

"I can't wait for recess," she said. "I really want to make it to spins this time. Do you think I will? I mean, if I don't mess up?"

I glanced at her, then pulled out my Wordly Wise workbook. "You shouldn't have worn a dress."

"Yeah, but look." She grabbed the hem of her dress and lifted it up, revealing a pair of white cotton shorts.

I yanked her hands away from her dress. "Dinah!"

Two rows back, Alex brayed his horsey laugh. "Did you see that?" he said to David May. He slapped his desk. "Man. I was really scared there for a second!"

"I've got to study my vocab," I told Dinah.

"But don't you want to help me practice? I know we don't have an actual rope, but we could—"

"I *said* I've got to study!"

She stared at me, wide-eyed, then twisted a piece of hair around her finger. I looked away, not wanting to see her pull it to her mouth.

"Are you mad at me?" she whispered.

I didn't answer.

"Because whatever I did, I'm really sorry." She hesitated. "Did I do something?"

Mr. Hutchinson strode into the room. "All right," he said. "Everyone to your seats."

"I'm not . . . mad," I said. "I just don't think we should do every single thing together all the time."

"Oh." She sucked on her hair. "I mean, you're right. It's dumb to practice during homeroom. I'll let you study, I promise."

"It's not that." I felt a tightening in my chest, and I couldn't meet her eyes. "I just mean in general. We shouldn't spend so much time together in general."

Dinah stood there.

"Peter?" Mr. Hutchinson said. "Dinah? We're waiting."

Finally, she turned and went to her seat.

"Who's first?" Louise said when we gathered on the playground. She pulled the Chinese jump rope from her backpack. "Should we do one potato, two potato?"

"I'm bored of Chinese jump rope," Gail said. She was wearing her Doc Martens again. "No offense, but aren't you guys getting a little sick of it?"

Louise paused.

Dinah glanced around the circle. She'd made a point of standing by Maxine and Lacey instead of with me, but I could see her alarm in the way she tugged at her dress. "Um, I'm not getting sick of it," she said. "I think we should play."

"And I think we shouldn't," Gail said with an edge. It was clear she was making this a battle, with everyone required to pick sides.

No one spoke. Silently, Louise put away the rope. I felt bad for Dinah, but what was I supposed to do? Louise had always been the bossiest girl in the grade, and even she couldn't stand up to Gail.

"Let's go watch the boys play basketball," Gail said. "We can do cheers."

"Sis boom bah," Chantelle chanted. "Rah, rah, rah!"

Amanda laughed—a little as if she were forcing it, but who was I to say?—and linked arms with both Chantelle and Gail. "Come on," she said to the rest of us. "It'll be fun."

We filed after her, everyone but Dinah. When I looked back from the basketball court, she was staring after us with her hands by her sides.

Gail taught us a cheer that involved clapping and knee-slapping in a complicated pattern. I tried to pay attention, but it was hard. My heart felt all scrunched up. Why did Gail have to win at everything? Even when she didn't win, she won. Why did she get to make the rules?

Amanda broke formation and came over to me. Her eyes flew to Dinah, and she lost her animated smile. "I know," she said awkwardly, even though I hadn't spoken.

I nodded.

She rubbed her thumb against one finger. "I feel sorry for her. I really do."

"Me, too," I whispered. But as I said it, I heard how horrible it sounded, and my heart scrunched another notch. Because *yes,* I did feel sorry for Dinah this very second, but that was only part of it. The rest was much, much bigger.

"Girls!" Gail said. She clapped twice to get everyone's attention. "Let's try it again, and this time let's give it our all." She put her hands on her hips like a squad captain. "Ready? O-kay!"

I took a shaky breath. Gail might have won over the others, but she wasn't in charge of me. No one was. And if I gave her that power anyway—her or Amanda or anyone—then *I* was the big loser. Not Dinah, but me.

Beside me, Amanda picked up the beat of the routine. "R-O-W-D-I-E! That's the way you spell *rowdy!* Row*dy!* Let's get row*dy!*"

Pulse thudding, I left the group. I walked toward Dinah and tried my best to act natural. But as I stood in front of her, my palms got all sweaty.

"Dinah . . ."

She looked as nervous as I was. When I didn't say anything, she licked her lips and said, "Do you, um, want to go swing?"

"Yeah," I said.

And we did.

February

Toby Rinehart is the absolute cutest boy in the world, even with pinkeye.

"Cuter than Robert Bond?" Dinah asked. Robert Bond has dimples when he smiles, which is pretty much all the time, and he likes to stand by the water fountain and splash the girls as they walk by. Practically everyone has a crush on him.

"Yep."

"Cuter than *Bo?*"

I was caught off guard. Dinah knew how I felt about Bo, and for her to bring him into the comparison was pret-ty tricky, I had to say. But I reminded myself that Bo was in the eleventh grade, not sixth, and anyway he's Sandra's boyfriend.

"Yep," I said, savoring Dinah's amazement. I looked across the room, to where Toby sat hunched over his desk drawing B-2 bombers in a spiral notebook. "His hair is so adorable, how it sticks up in the back. And his eyes. He's got the most beautiful eyes, don't you think?"

"They're pink," Dinah said.

"Exactly the color of candy hearts."

"He's got pinkeye, Winnie."

"Yeah, but it's viral, not bacterial, so he's not contagious."
I sighed. "He said the only way I could catch it would be to
press my eyeball right up next to his."

Dinah giggled. "You are moony, Winifred Perry."

It was true. I was. Valentine's Day was less than twenty-
four hours away, and I'd picked Toby to be my one-and-only.
The problem now was getting him to pick me back. At the
beginning of the week, Tyrone had asked Chantelle to go
with him ("Go *where?*" Dinah said, and I'd hid my face in
my hands), and in the following three days, three more couples had paired up: Louise and Grant, David and Karen, and
Peter and Sheila.

I wanted to be the next girl asked. Or not even next, just
so long as I wasn't left high and dry at ten-thirty tomorrow
morning, when the three sixth-grade classes would get
together to drop Valentines into our homemade boxes. Last
year, I got fifteen cards, which was good, but they were all
the white punch-out kind with Snoopy on them or Donald
Duck. This year, I was hoping for Hallmark.

During language arts, Mr. Hutchinson divided the class in
half and let us call out words to prepare for Friday's spelling
test. When it was my turn, I called on Toby and gave him
an easy one: *kinship.* Spelling isn't Toby's best subject, but

kinship had only two syllables, and all the vowels sounded the way they should.

"K-I-N-S-H-I-P," Toby said.

Mr. Hutchinson chalked up a point for their team, and Maxine said, "Winnie! Don't you even *want* to win?"

I shrugged and kept my eyes on Toby, but he was slapping hands with Peter and didn't notice. Then Karen called on me with *abrupt,* which I accidentally put two *b*s in.

"Yes!" Toby said, making a fist and pulling it in at his side. "Seven to five!"

I sank down in my seat, and Dinah patted my hand.

During lunch, I waited until Toby was watching, then wandered to the sharing table and placed my Snickers beside a brown banana and half of a smushed PB&J. "Guess I don't want this Snickers after all," I said. "Oh, well. Guess I'll just—"

Toby, Peter, and Alex leapt from their chairs and raced for the table.

"Mine!" Alex gloated, grabbing the Snickers and clutching it to his chest. "Ha, ha! Unless maybe I change my mind . . ." He dropped the Snickers on the sharing table for less than a second, then snatched it back. "Not!"

Peter scowled, and Toby looked at me like it was my fault. Like if I'd put it closer to the edge, he'd probably have gotten there first.

I blinked and peered into my lunch bag. "Guess I'll give

up these carrots, too," I said, pulling out a wilted plastic bag. I smiled hopefully at Toby. "Anyone want some carrots?"

Alex unwrapped the Snickers and crammed half of it in his mouth. He waved the uneaten half in front of Peter and Toby and sang, "Thank you, Winnie."

By recess, I was beginning to feel desperate. Not only had Toby scooted away his desk when I tried to help him with his social studies, but when I raised my hand and asked if the Aztecs ever got pinkeye, he blushed and stared at the floor. And when I stood next to him by the water fountain and said, "*Please* don't splash me with the water," he got all fidgety and hurried away. I was beginning to think he was avoiding me.

"Oh, I don't know," Dinah said. "Maybe he's just shy."

I dug the toe of my sneaker into the dirt and leaned sideways, twisting my swing in a circle. "Why, though? Doesn't he know I like him?"

"Who?" Gail said, strolling over with Chantelle. "Doesn't *who* know you like him?"

"No one," I said.

Gail turned to Dinah. "Come on, tell us who you're talking about."

Dinah chewed on a strand of hair.

"Fine," Gail said. "Have your little secrets."

I lifted my legs and let my swing unwind. "What about you, Gail?" I said when I stopped moving. "You still like Ross Gallivan?"

Gail turned red. On Tuesday, she'd slipped an anonymous love letter into Ross's lunch box, only everyone knew it was her because of how it smelled. She'd sprayed perfume all over it, thick, flowery perfume that clung to her backpack as well.

"That was a joke, Winnie," she said. "Obviously."

I raised my eyebrows. She was just saying that because Ross tossed the letter into the trash. He threw away most of his lunch, too, wrinkling his nose and complaining of the stink. But Gail wanted a boyfriend as much as the rest of us. I could see it in the way her eyes kept flitting to the opposite side of the playground, where Ross goofed around with some of his friends.

"Anyway," she said, "why would I write a love letter to Ross Gallivan? A boy in my condominium complex already asked if I'd be his Valentine, and I said yes." She folded her arms across her chest. "He's thirteen."

Chantelle looked at Gail in surprise, then caught me watching and quickly fixed her expression. "It's true," she said. "Yesterday he gave her a bouquet of roses, just because it's *almost* Valentine's Day. Right, Gail?"

"That's right," Gail said, but her lips got thin as if she knew Chantelle had gone too far.

"Uh-huh," I said.

A squeal caught our attention, and we turned to see Amanda dashing toward us. "Guess what, guess what?" she said.

"Robert asked me to go with him! We were in the library help-ing Mrs. Grady, and he pulled me behind the dinosaur display and asked me, just like that. I can't believe it!"

"Amanda, that's awesome!" Chantelle said. She threw her arms around her, and the two of them hopped up and down. "That means we can go shopping this afternoon for Valentine's cards! And on Friday, we can sit together at the couples' table!"

The *couples'* table? I didn't know anything about a cou-ples' table. One glance at Gail told me that she didn't, either.

"What's the couples' table?" Dinah asked.

Chantelle and Amanda looked at each other and giggled.

"You tell them," Chantelle said.

"No, you."

"You."

Gail breathed out through her nose, and Amanda made herself stop laughing.

"It's nothing, really," she said. "It's just that all the cou-ples are going to sit together on Valentine's Day, and Louise is going to bring pink lemonade and sugar cookies shaped like hearts." She shrugged, as if she suddenly realized that the rest of us might not be as excited as she and Chantelle were. "I just found out about it this morning."

"Oh," Dinah said. "Is she bringing cookies for the rest of us, too?"

"Just the couples," Chantelle said.

Gail's eyes met with mine, and for the briefest second I knew we were thinking the same thing: that the couples' table was a horrible idea. Worse than either of us could have imagined.

Then she tossed her hair over her shoulders and said, "Well, I think that's sweet. Brett, my boyfriend, is going to make me an entire Valentine's Day dinner, whatever I request. We're going to eat on the patio, under the light of the moon."

"Brett?" Amanda said. "Who's Brett?"

I stood up from my swing. "Come on, Dinah," I said. "Let's go."

During science, when Ms. Gardner was out of the room, David and Karen held hands across the smooth, pale table while Alex counted out loud. They made it to a hundred and five before the sound of footsteps sent everyone scurrying back to their seats. Rory Johnson was so impressed that he asked Tamela Chaddock to go with him on the spot, and she grinned and said yes. Louise uncapped her pen and made a note in her spiral.

And five minutes before class let out, Karen leaned over to me and whispered, "Can you make your eyes smile without moving your mouth?"

"I don't know," I said. I sat up straight and concentrated hard inside my brain. "There. Could you tell?"

"You look like you have to go to the bathroom."

Any other day, I would have scowled and turned back to my science book. But today I was so glad to be talking about something other than Valentine's Day that I overlooked her remark and said, "Well, can you?"

"Nope. But David, my boyfriend, can. He just thinks of something he really likes—like me, for example—and his eyes get all twinkly." She studied me, tilting her head. "Now it looks like you *really* have to go to the bathroom."

After the bell rang, I joined Dinah outside, and we sat down to wait for our carpools.

"This is terrible," I said. "We're going to be the only ones sitting alone tomorrow. You know that, don't you? There all the couples will be, munching away on their stupid heart cookies, and there we'll be, eating our normal, boring lunches all by ourselves. Just you and me."

"And Gail," Dinah said.

I groaned.

"And Maxine. And Lacey. And Cara. She's not going with anyone, I'm pretty sure."

"Not the point," I said. "The point is . . . the point is that tomorrow is Valentine's Day. You're supposed to get candy and flowers and big, glossy cards, not just your everyday bologna sandwich."

"We could trade if you want," Dinah said. "I could pack something for you, and you could pack something for me. Then when we traded, it would be a surprise."

I unzipped my backpack and tore a piece of paper from my notebook. I scribbled a note, folded it over, and gave it to Dinah. "Here. Deliver this to Toby. Quick, before his ride shows up."

She looked at me uncertainly.

"Please! It's important!"

She bit her lip and walked across the parking lot. She handed the note to Peter, Toby's best friend, and Peter passed it to Toby. My heart thumped, and I stared really hard at my feet. A few seconds later, Dinah's Keds whapped against the asphalt, and she thrust the note in front of me.

"Here," she panted. "Read it!"

I glanced across the parking lot. Peter smirked, hands in his pockets, while Toby shoved him and tried to make him turn around.

"*Read* it!" Dinah said.

I opened the note. *Dear Toby,* it said. *Do you like Winnie?* Underneath, I'd put three boxes: yes, no, and maybe. Toby had checked "maybe."

Dinah did a series of tiny, excited claps.

"Winnie, that's awesome! 'Maybe' is practically the same as 'yes,' and that practically guarantees he's going to ask you to go with him!"

I checked my watch, thinking again of tomorrow's card exchange. "Yeah, well, he's got nineteen and a half hours to do it. Actually less, because I'm not allowed to talk on the phone after eight."

I hugged my knees to my chest. I imagined pulling an oversize Hallmark from my Valentine's box, one with a sunset on the front, or a seagull flying over the ocean. Or maybe one of those with a lift-up flap of cellophane, to make it look dreamy and elegant. Then I imagined myself at the couples' table, heart-shaped cookie in one hand, a fancy glass of lemonade in the other.

Maybe.

That afternoon I watched *Oprah* with Sandra. The topic was "High School Sweethearts Reunited," and one guest proposed on the air by giving his old girlfriend a bouquet of roses with a ring in the middle. It was so sweet. During a commercial, I asked Sandra what she and Bo were doing for Valentine's Day.

"Going to the Melting Pot for chocolate fondue," she said. "And then downtown to take a horse-and-carriage ride. Mom's letting me borrow that soft red sweater of hers, and she's going to French-braid my hair."

I scooched lower on the sofa. Sandra looked beautiful with her hair French braided. "Are you guys going to get married, do you think?"

She snorted. "Not tomorrow."

"But someday?"

"I have no idea. Why?"

"I don't know. It just . . . it must be so nice to have a boyfriend."

Sandra hit the "mute" button on the remote. She eye-balled me from beneath her bangs. "You have a crush on someone, don't you? You *do!* Because tomorrow's Valentine's Day, and everyone's supposed to pass out cards." She nodded. "I remember."

"Not *just* because of that," I said.

"Uh-huh. How many kids have already paired up?"

"Twelve."

"Twelve? When I was in sixth grade, everyone in the class was going steady. Everyone but Chelsea Dunmeyer." She drummed her fingers. "Still, you don't want to be one of the girls left out, no matter how many of you there are."

I waited, grateful that Sandra was taking this seriously. When I asked Mom how to go about getting a guy's attention, she suggested studying for my decimals test, since everyone's wowed by good math skills.

Oprah came back on, and Sandra picked up the remote. "Well, good luck."

My mouth fell open. "Good luck? That's all you're going to say?"

"What do you want me to say?"

"But he hasn't asked me to go with him yet. And after tomorrow it'll be too late!"

"So ask him yourself. Now, shh! I'm trying to watch!"

For the rest of the show I considered her remark. And afterward, when I went upstairs to do the Valentine's Day crossword puzzle Mr. Hutchinson gave us for homework, I kept on considering it. Because really, there was no reason I couldn't ask Toby to go with me, if that's what I wanted to do. Just because nobody else had the guts to ask a guy didn't mean I shouldn't, either. Where would the world be without Amelia Earhart? Or Madame Curie?

I marched across the hall to Ty's bedroom. "Get up," I said, grabbing his arm and pulling him away from his Rescue Heroes. "There's something very important I need to do, and you have to help me."

"Is it a raid?" Ty said. He swooshed Jake Justice through the air and made siren sounds.

"No, not a raid. It's . . . a reconnaissance mission. Come on!"

In the kitchen, I flipped open the school directory and ran my finger down the sixth-grade class list. I punched in Toby's number and handed the phone to Ty.

"What am I supposed to say?" he said.

"Ask to speak to Toby. And then ask if he wants to go with me."

"Go where?"

"Nowhere. Just ask him."

"But how will he—" He clutched the phone to his ear, then widened his eyes. He banged the phone down in the cradle.

"Ty! Why'd you do that?"

"Someone answered!"

"Well, of *course* someone answered! That's why it's called a *phone!*" I picked up the phone and hit the redial button. "Here, try again. Don't hang up!"

He swallowed, fingers tight around the receiver. "Hello?" he said. "May I please speak to Toby?"

I got beside him and put my ear next to his. I heard voices in the background, plus a rustling sound like someone was eating potato chips out of a bag. Then footsteps, followed by a careful "Hello?"

I dug my elbow into Ty's ribs.

"Uh, Winnie wants to know if you want to go to the mall," he said.

"Not the *mall!*" I whispered.

"The mall?" Toby said.

I shook head frantically.

"No," Ty said. "The, uh . . . the—" He banged down the phone.

"Ty!"

"I couldn't help it!"

"Just ask if he wants to go with me. That's all!" Once more I hit the redial button and put the receiver between our ears.

"Hello?" someone said after only one ring. Whoever it was sounded older, like maybe Toby's brother. And he sounded mad.

Ty gulped. "May I . . . speak to Toby?"

"No. And tell your sister to leave him alone. He's not interested!" And then *he* banged down the phone.

Ty stared at me.

I stared back. My legs and stomach felt shaky, like the time Dad yelled at me for breaking his camera, which I wasn't supposed to be playing with in the first place. Only this was worse, because I didn't even know I was doing something bad until Toby's brother exploded.

"Winnie?" Ty pleaded in a tiny voice.

I blinked hard to push back my tears. Ty's hand snaked out to grab the bottom of my T-shirt—something he used to do when he was a baby—but I shook him off and ran to my room.

"Nice outfit," Louise said the next morning in homeroom.

I looked down at my black pants and black *Phantom of the Opera* shirt, then back at Louise in her pink flowered jumper.

"Valentine's Day is for soft hearts and soft minds," I announced loftily.

That's what Sandra had said last night, to comfort me after hearing what happened with Toby. She'd rubbed my back and told one embarrassing story after another, all about things she'd done when *she* was eleven.

"Anyway, that guy was a jerk," she'd said, referring to Toby's brother. "He can only make you feel bad if you let him." She'd said it didn't matter anyway, since Toby was just a Valentine's Day crush and in a week I'd no longer care. Which was probably true, but I didn't like having it pointed out like that.

Louise gazed at me pityingly. "Grant gave me three red roses," she said. "Want to see?"

I stomped to my desk.

When Dinah arrived, I was busy scribbling in letters on my crossword puzzle, which I never finished the night before. At least, I was pretending to be busy. Toby's desk sat empty in the back of the room, and I didn't want him to think I cared when he finally showed up.

"So?" Dinah said, plunking down beside me. "Did Toby call? Did he ask you to go with him?"

"I took the phone off the hook," I said. I'd gotten scared that Toby's brother might use star-six-nine and call me back, so I slipped Mom and Dad's bedroom phone off the hang-up button and acted as confused as everyone else when Sandra couldn't get a dial tone.

"But I thought you wanted him to call," Dinah said.

I shrugged.

David May sauntered to our desks, the Hershey bar Karen had given him sticking out of his shirt pocket. "Hi, girls," he said.

"Hi yourself," I said back. If he started flaunting that Hershey bar around, I was going to kick him.

He turned to Dinah. "Alex wants to know if you'll go with him, and you better say yes, because no one else is going to ask you."

"Ex*cuse* me?!" I said. "Well, tell Alex to go jump in a lake. Right, Dinah?"

Dinah giggled and pressed her hand to her mouth.

I lifted my eyebrows. "*Right,* Dinah?"

"Well?" David said.

"Okay," Dinah said. "I'll go with him."

I gaped at her.

David tugged something free from his pocket. "Here. He said to give you this."

I lunged for the small white envelope, but Dinah beat me to it. She gave me a sheepish smile.

"But it's not even ten-thirty!" I said. "And plus, he's supposed to put it in your box, not just—" A movement behind her caught my attention. Toby, coming in at last. His pinkeye had disappeared from his right eye, but had worsened in his left, making it look bulgy and raw. He paused in the doorway, then spotted me and started across the room.

"Oh, no," I said.

"What?" Dinah asked.

I jerked up the crossword puzzle and held it two inches in front of my face. I tried to breathe.

"Winnie," Dinah said.

I ignored her.

"Winnie!"

I lowered the ditto a fraction of an inch. Toby stood before me, hands jammed under his arms.

"Did you make your little brother call me last night?" he said.

My face went hot. "No."

"You didn't?"

"I didn't *make* him. He wanted to."

Toby kicked at the floor. "It's just that he kept hanging up, and my brother got kind of mad."

I swallowed. I could feel Dinah listening, and that wasn't so bad, but David was there, too, and I knew it would be all over the school by lunchtime. It would be worse than Gail and the smelly letter.

"But I didn't tell him to say that, at the end," Toby said.

"Say what?" David said.

I lifted my head. "You didn't?"

"Say *what?*" David said.

"Nothing!" Toby and I said together.

He uncrossed his arms and handed me a wrinkled white envelope, the same size as the one David gave Dinah. It was slightly damp, but I didn't care.

"I know we're supposed to wait, but—"

I waved my fingers in the air. "That's all right."

He turned to leave.

"Toby, wait. I, um . . . I guess I was just wondering." My heart thumped. "Do you want to go with me?"

Beside me, Dinah squealed.

"Well?" David said. "Answer her, man."

Toby rubbed his eye with his fist, then dropped his hand to his side. "I guess so," he said. He nodded. "All right."

That afternoon at the couples' table, the girls compared cards while the boys zinged each other with Louise's heart-shaped cookies. Amanda's card from Robert played "Bicycle Built for Two" when she lifted the front flap, and we took turns opening and shutting it until finally she made us stop. Ross, who asked Gail to go with him five minutes before lunch began, had drawn a robot with the head of a fly on a piece of notebook paper, with HAPPY VALENTINE'S DAY coming out of its mouth. Gail told us the card meant even more since it was homemade, but later she just happened to knock over her drink carton, spilling grape juice all over her sandwich *and* Ross's drawing.

"Oh, no!" she cried. "Look what I've done!"

Dinah's card from Alex was a white punch-out with Bart Simpson on the front. *Don't have a cow,* it said. *Be my valentine!*

"I know it's kind of obnoxious," Dinah said, blushing and looping a strand of hair around one finger. "But it's funny, too. Don't you think?"

I'd gotten a Simpson's card from Toby as well, only mine

had a picture of Lisa playing her trombone. I didn't rub it in to Dinah, but secretly I was pleased. I'd seen the Simpsons' cards in the drugstore, and in a box of twenty, there were ten Barts, five Homers, and five assorted extras. Of those five, only one showed Lisa with her trombone.

March

IT WAS THE BEGINNING OF MARCH, and the days were getting warmer. Mr. Hutchinson decorated our bulletin board with the delicate gauze butterflies we made in art. In science, Ms. Gardner showed time-lapse photography films of tulips and daffodils opening to the sun. And during lunch we were tipsy with spring fever, calling out to friends at other tables, tossing food back and forth, and—in my case—making excited plans about my birthday, which was less than two weeks away.

Last year, it was Amanda and I who giggled together, discussing pizza versus hamburgers, chocolate cake versus rainbow swirl. This year it was Dinah who sat beside me, nodding eagerly as I told her about Benihana's, the restaurant I'd invited her to for the night of my birthday itself. Sandra said you got to take your shoes off and eat at these special tables that were really low to the ground. You didn't use chairs; you just sat on the floor. Then the chef came and did all kinds of cool knife stuff right in front of you.

"I love fancy dinners," Dinah said. "I love how grown-up they make you feel. Is it just going to be the two of us?"

"Plus my mom and dad and Sandra and Ty," I said. "But yeah, other than my family, it'll just be us two."

I looked at her, and for a moment I fell silent. It was weird realizing how much things had changed in just one year. Not bad, just . . . weird. But mainly it was exhilarating, thinking about all the fun we were going to have.

"I know!" Dinah said. "Maybe before dinner we could play games, to work up our appetites. Maybe Chinese jump rope. Do you think?"

I swatted her. She was still obsessed with Chinese jump rope, and I know she hoped it would regain favor on the playground. But it never did. "How are we supposed to play Chinese jump rope with just two people, you dope?"

"Well, for the third player we could use a chair, and loop the jump rope around its legs. That would work!"

"Maybe," I said.

"Then your birthday would have a theme," she said, "because first we'd play Chinese jump rope and then we'd eat at that Chinese restaurant, Benihoohoo's or whatever."

I acted all offended. "It's Beni*hana's*, Dinah. Please. And it's Japanese, not Chinese, all right?"

"But . . . I don't know how to play Japanese jump rope," Dinah said.

We both cracked up, because it sounded so silly: Japanese jump rope. Amanda, who was on her way back from getting her milk, paused by our table and said, "Hey, you two. What's so funny?"

"Nothing," I said.

"Benihoohoo's," Dinah whispered, and we got all chortle-y again.

"Huh?" Amanda said.

I made myself calm down. "We were just talking about my birthday, that's all."

"Oh, yeah? Are you going to have a pizza party again?"

My laughter dried up for real as I grasped what I'd just walked into. I searched for an acceptable answer, but my brain was frozen. "Um, well . . ."

"Her mom said no big party," Dinah said. "This year it's Sandra's turn, and next month Sandra's going to have her whole class spend the night to celebrate turning sixteen. Well, not the boys, obviously. Anyway, Winnie's mom says that that's enough stress to last a lifetime."

I balled up my napkin. I didn't know if Dinah was as oblivious to the situation as she was acting, or if she was chattering on and on *because* of how awkward it was.

"So you don't get to have a party at all?" Amanda said. "That's so unfair!"

Dinah glanced at me, and I could tell by her expression that she *did* get it. I could have said nothing—just let Amanda keep thinking what she already thought—and Dinah would have understood. But that would have been like hiding Dinah's and my friendship, and I'd done that too much already.

"Mom and Dad are taking me out for a fancy dinner," I said in a small voice. A knot formed in my stomach. "I only get to invite one friend."

Amanda scrunched her forehead, maybe wondering why I was only now telling her. Then she understood. She blushed. "Oh."

"Yeah. I, um, kind of invited Dinah."

She nodded to show she'd figured that out. "That's great."

"But I didn't . . . I mean, I never meant to—"

"No, really. That's awesome. I'll, you know, probably be doing something with Gail that night anyway."

She gave me a lopsided smile, which after a moment I returned. A look passed between us that made my heart hurt.

"What's going on?" Gail demanded, approaching our table. She eyed me and Dinah suspiciously. "Amanda, aren't you coming?"

"I'll be there in a second," Amanda said.

"You have to come *now*," Gail said. "Robert says he's going to eat your brownie if you don't claim it."

"So let him," Amanda said. "Anyway, it's all dry and crumbly." But she followed Gail toward their table.

"Bye," Dinah said softly.

Amanda didn't hear her, but Gail did, and she blasted Dinah with her glare. Dinah drew back, and I slowly exhaled.

᪣ ᪣ ᪣

Usually during recess we run off in groups of two or three and do whatever we want, but sometimes, like today, all the girls clustered near the swing set and came up with ideas together.

"Let's work on our cartwheels," Louise suggested. Louise took gymnastics lessons after school and she was always wanting to show off.

"Excuse me, but no," Gail said.

"Why not?" asked Louise.

Gail rolled her eyes and gestured to her outfit, which consisted of a short blue skirt and a white shirt.

My thought was, *Well, you shouldn't have worn such a short skirt.* But Louise looked embarrassed and said, "Oh. Right."

Gail examined her nails. "Plus, and I don't mean to be rude, but . . ."

"What?"

Gail shot a sideways glance at Dinah. She still had it out for her, which I didn't understand. Sometimes I thought it was actually me she didn't like, only she couldn't be too mean to me because of Amanda, so she picked on Dinah as the next best thing.

At any rate, she turned back to Louise and said, "It's just that a few of us have talked about it, and it's really kind of embarrassing the way certain people bounce around, especially when they're not wearing a bra. Especially with the boys right near by."

Dinah blushed, but she wasn't the only one. As far as I knew, lots of the girls in our grade didn't wear a bra. I sure didn't.

Did Gail? I checked her shoulder. Under her shirt was a strap-size ridge.

"I know, let's play Truth or Dare," she proclaimed. "It'll give us practice for junior high." She scanned the circle. "Chantelle. Truth or Dare?"

"Me? Uh, truth. No, dare! No, truth." She covered her face with her hands. "Truth."

"Who do you think is the hottest boy in the grade?"

I let out my breath, which I hadn't realized I'd been holding. With the mood Gail was in, I guess I'd been afraid she would ask something embarrassing, or something not very nice. But asking Chantelle who she thought was hot was like asking a teacher if we really needed to learn math. Everyone knew exactly what she'd say.

"That's easy," Chantelle said. "Tyrone Williams. And now it's my turn, right?" She tapped her finger against her lip. "Okay, Lacey. Truth or dare?"

"Truth."

"Did you *really* go on the Scream Machine sixteen times when your uncle took you to Six Flags?"

Lacey's mouth dropped open, and everyone laughed. "I did!" she protested. "You can ask my uncle!"

Lacey asked Maxine if she still wore days-of-the-week underwear, and Maxine, after making a face and saying no, asked Cara if she'd marry Mr. Hutchinson, if she were old enough and if Mr. Hutchinson proposed. And Louise, one of the few people to take a dare, skipped around the basketball court singing the *Sesame Street* song, just because Cara said she had to.

I laughed along with the others, and when Sheila dared me to climb to the top of the swing set, I shimmied up the pole in fifteen seconds flat, then slid back down like a firefighter heading for a rescue. Everyone cheered, and I grinned and flexed my arms. My biceps were like small, hard eggs.

But then the questions got trickier, like have you ever held hands with a boy or have you ever kissed a boy, things like that. My body tensed, although I tried not to let it show.

Gail, however, was loving it. "Yeah, right," she said when Louise bragged about holding Grant's hand on our field trip to the planetarium. "Then why didn't anyone see?"

"Because it was dark," Louise said.

"Not that dark," Gail replied.

And when Cara mumbled that she might have kissed a boy, but she wasn't one hundred percent positive, Gail snorted like that was the dumbest thing she'd ever heard. "Either you kissed him or you didn't," Gail said. "Unless . . . oh, God. You're not talking about your dad or your brother or someone, are you? Because that does *not* count as a kiss, Cara, unless you're more desperate than I thought."

The rest of us giggled nervously. Dinah, too, although she

shouldn't have, because Gail turned at the sound of her voice. The way she gazed at her made my throat close.

"All right, Dinah," she said. "Truth or dare?"

Dinah stopped giggling. "But, um, it's not your turn. It's Cara's."

"Cara doesn't mind," Gail said. "Do you, Cara?"

Cara blinked. She inched backward.

"Now, truth or dare?" Gail asked Dinah. "Or are you too much of a baby?"

Color rose in Dinah's cheeks. "I guess truth," she whispered.

"What?"

"Truth."

"All right, all right! I'm not deaf, you know."

Dinah hugged her arms around her ribs, and I saw her shiver. I wished we were anywhere but here.

"So," Gail said. "Dinah. Not counting your father, and not counting any other relative like a grandfather or an uncle or a nephew, have *you* ever kissed a boy?"

Dinah's hand crept toward her mouth. She chewed her thumbnail.

"Have you?" Gail demanded.

Dinah took her thumb away from her mouth. "Alex Plotkin," she said in a wavery voice. "On Valentine's Day. He kissed me in the parking lot, after school let out."

My stomach dropped. On Valentine's Day, Dinah had

come home with me. Together we left the building, and together we waited by the curb for Mom to arrive.

"He did not," Gail said.

"He did, too!"

Gail arched her eyebrows. She pivoted toward the basketball court and called, "Alex! Could you come here, please?"

"Gail . . ." Amanda said uneasily.

"What? I just want to ask him if it's true."

Some of the girls exchanged nervous glances, but no one spoke out.

Alex crossed the playground, along with David, Peter, and Toby. Dinah tensed beside me. Her eyes flew to mine.

"What's up?" Alex asked.

"We just have a question for you," Gail said. "We just want to know if you—"

"No!" I cried. My heart whammed in my chest, but I made myself step forward. "No one cares who somebody kissed or didn't kiss, so just shut up, okay?"

"What are you talking about?" Alex said. "Who kissed who?"

"No one," I said. "No one kissed anyone, but that's not the point."

"Then what *is* the point, Winnie?" Gail asked.

"The point . . ." I said. "The point is . . ."

She smirked.

"The point is that you are not the boss of things just because you wear a bra!"

Eleven

David and Peter hooted, and Alex cackled his horsey laug

"A *bra!*" he crowed. "You're not the boss of things because you wear a *bra!*"

"A feminine support garment," said David.

"An over-the-shoulder-boulder-holder!" said Peter.

Gail turned bright red. She glared and said, "You're just jealous because you *don't!*"

"She is not," Dinah said, moving up beside me. She linked her arm through mine.

"A brassiere," Toby said in a phony French accent.

Lacey and Maxine snickered because he sounded so dumb.

"It's not funny," Gail said. "I *said* it's not funny! Anyway, laughing causes wrinkles!"

"Oh, please," Lacey said. She broke free from the circle. "I'm going to play on the balance beam. Maxine, want to come?"

"Sure," Maxine said.

Karen hesitated for a moment, then hurried after them. "Hey, wait for me!"

The guys headed back toward the basketball court, shoving one another and making more bra jokes. Cara and Sheila wandered to the jungle gym, while Chantelle and Louise hovered near Gail, reassuring her with pats and quick words.

Dinah's body relaxed against me. First she giggled, and then I joined in, as giddiness filled us up. Amanda looked at the two of us, and for a second I thought she was going to come over. But Gail clutched her sleeve, and she turned away.

❧ ❧ ❧

, Dinah came over after lunch. She found me up

bedroom, and I dumped Sweetie-Pie out of my lap and

ged on my sneakers. Sweetie-Pie meowed in complaint,

and I went back to the bed and gave her a quick pet. "Silly

cat," I told her. "I can't spend every minute with you, you

goof!" I scratched her behind the ears, and then Dinah and

I ran downstairs and told Sandra and Bo we were ready.

"Can't you get Mom or Dad to drive you?" Sandra said.

"We're in the middle of *Sponge Bob*."

I grabbed the remote and switched off the TV. "You prom-

ised you'd take us. Come on."

At Toys "R" Us, Dinah and I each bought our very own

Chinese jump rope, and in the back of Bo's Jeep, we ripped

off the plastic packaging and stretched them between our

hands.

"What are you going to do with those?" Bo said. "Shoot a

giant spitball?"

I looked at Dinah and swiveled my finger by my temple.

She tittered.

"They're Chinese jump ropes," I said. "You use them to

play Chinese jump rope."

"Oh-h-h," Bo said. "So, what, you have to do everything

upside down?"

"Ha, ha. When we get home, we'll show you. You guys

can help us practice, because next Friday is my birthday and

we'll probably play Chinese jump rope before we go to dinner. If you're really, really nice, I might even let Sandra
invite you."

"What do you mean 'might'?" Bo said. He caught my eye
in the rearview mirror. "How old are you going to be, anyway? Eighteen? Nineteen?"

"For your information, I'm going to be twelve, thank you
very much."

"Wow," Sandra said, "twelve whole years. Pretty impres-
sive."

I leaned back, propping my feet on Bo's seat. "You got that
right."

Out in the backyard, while Dad pruned the boxwoods
and Mom read her mystery in a stretched-out chaise longue,
Sandra, Bo, and Ty played Chinese jump rope with me and
Dinah. Sandra was as bad at "scoop" as I was, but Dinah
taught us a trick that made it easier.

"Pretend your foot is a fork and the rope is a spaghetti
noodle," she said. "Just scoop it up like it was the last noodle on the plate. Then when you jump, point your foot, and
the rope will slide right off."

"Oh, sure," I said. "Easy for you to say."

"You can do it," Dinah said. "Now *go!*"

I hooked the rope over the toe of my sneaker and leapt
into the air.